Mirror Lake Press

Cover design by Lisa Messagee
Interior design by Heather Justesen

Print ISBN-13: 978-1537151779
Print ISBN-10: 1537151770

Acknowledgements

As always, I owe my sincerest thanks to my critique partners, Jennifer Griffith and Joyce DiPastena who are so encouraging as well as willing to point out all the ways my story could be improved. Thank you, too, to my Beta readers—Karen Adair, Heidi Murphy, Tracy Astle, Rebecca Barrett, Shaunna Gonzales, and Pauline Hansen. And thank you to my final proofreaders, Susie Hatch, Charlotte Morgan, Debbie DeTemple and Julie Moody. I couldn't have done it without all of you!

Also my gratitude goes to my ANWA sister-writers, and the members of the Beau Monde RWA writers group.

A special thanks to musician extraordinaire, Jenna Hartley, for her feedback on a musician's life in a professional orchestra.

And, lastly, I must thank my husband and children who are tirelessly supportive, even though they sometimes have to deal with pancakes for dinner because I didn't come out of my writing coma in time to prepare a nutritious meal. I love you!

Other titles by Donna Hatch:

The Rogue Hearts Regency Series:
The Stranger She Married, book 1
The Guise of a Gentleman, book 2
A Perfect Secret, book 3
The Suspect's Daughter, book 4

Anthologies:
Timeless Romance, *Winter Collection* "A Winter's Knight"
Timeless Regency Romance, *Autumn Masquerade* "Unmasking the Duke"
Timeless Regency Romance, *Summer House Party* "A Perfect Match"
With Every Heartbeat, "The Reluctant Bride," Emma's Dilemma," "Constant Hearts"

Heart Strings, Songs of the Heart series Book 1
Courting the Countess: Coming October 2016

Novellas and Short Stories:
"When Ship Bells Ring"
"Constant Hearts"
"Emma's Dilemma"
"The Reluctant Bride"
"Troubled Hearts"

Christmas Novellas:
"A Winter's Knight"
"A Christmas Reunion"
"Mistletoe Magic"

Fantasy Novel:
Queen in Exile

DISCLAIMER

Every possible measure has been taken to insure this book is free of grammatical, typographical, and formatting errors. Please forgive those few that may have slipped past the many, many eyes that searched for them.

Chapter One

England, 1811

From the time Susanna Dyer was orphaned at the age of thirteen, she had known she was unwanted, but each time her aunt vocalized that truth, Susanna couldn't refrain from wincing. Even now, at nineteen, she battled to maintain composure during her aunt's "talks." Susanna stood in her aunt's morning room—formerly her mother's morning room—her head demurely bowed and her hands clasped, when every muscle in her body strained to run out of range from the verbal arrows Aunt Uriana continued to shoot at her.

Her aunt, sitting against her pillows like a queen, paused after extolling all of Susanna's faults before declaring, "But, at last, I have found the perfect solution. My nephew on *my* side of the family—" this spoken as if her side of the family were irrefutably superior to her husband's side of the family—"a paragon of gentlemanly virtue, has agreed to marry you for the sake of your dowry, however small, to satisfy his patron's requirement that he be wedded in order to assume the position as vicar."

Forgoing her study of the faded scarlet carpeting, Susanna lifted her head. "Your nephew? Not Algernon Bloodworth?"

Aunt Uriana let out a huff and rolled her eyes. "Of course, Algernon. I only have one nephew on my side of the family, you half-witted buffoon."

Perfect. She was to marry a man sixteen years her senior with gout, a propensity to whistle when he breathed, a wit as sharp as a wet bar of soap, and a cruel streak—the kind that drowned kittens and kicked puppies. Oh, and this so-called "paragon of gentlemanly virtue" only wanted her so he could assume a position—as a vicar, no less. Susanna would have to sign her name *Mrs. Bloodworth*. She shivered, almost as repulsed by his name as by his character.

Truly fate must be cackling at this point.

She couldn't help repeating, on the off-chance that she'd misheard her aunt. "You want me to marry your nephew, Algernon Bloodworth?"

Aunt Uriana let out a long-suffering sigh as if she were speaking to a rather trying, stupid child, and nodded, making her double chin bulge more than normal. "Yes!"

"But he's so..." Susanna settled on the least offensive word she could, "...old."

Aunt Uriana made an impatient sound. "He's only thirty-five—still in his prime. It's the perfect

2

solution. I finally get rid of you. He gets appointed to the position he desires."

The walls closed in and all light dimmed in the room. For a moment, Susanna could hardly breathe. Trapped in a marriage with a troll of a man. No. Never.

With uncharacteristic boldness, Susanna asked, "Does Uncle approve of this match?"

Aunt Uriana opened her mouth in shock. "How dare you question me? Of course he approves. Algernon is my nephew, after all."

Wearily, Susanna nodded. From the time her papa's brother arrived to take possession of the entailed property and guardianship of Susanna, he'd never once contradicted Aunt. If he held any opinions, he kept them to himself, probably for the sake of his version of peace.

Susanna took a breath, swallowed, took another. For the first time in years, she made a stand. "I thank you for your kind offer, Aunt." She nearly choked on the words. "However, I must decline."

"*What?*" Aunt Uriana's eyes bulged. "What did you say to me? You most assuredly do not decline. I am your guardian until you marry, and I refuse to keep you under my roof any longer than necessary. I won't allow you, with your stupid, backward ways and the idiotic things you say, to ruin my daughter's chances

3

for an advantageous marriage. As soon as you are gone, I will bring her 'out' and we will attend London for her first Season. The best part is, I won't have to worry about you any longer."

This implied her aunt had ever worried about Susanna. Of course, she didn't voice that thought. Instead, Susanna called forth her most respectful, sweet tone of voice. "You could simply leave me behind while you go to London, Aunt—no need to find me a husband first."

"Algernon needs a wife and he has agreed to take *you*." Her upper lip curled as if she found the thought distasteful. "Now, leave." Aunt Uriana made a shooing motion which set the fat hanging from her arms to shaking, and picked up her embroidery loom.

Susanna's breath came in shallow spurts. She could not marry Algernon. Could not! She squared her shoulders. "No, Aunt."

Aunt Uriana lowered her embroidery loom and leveled a stare at her that would have frozen the Thames. She punctuated each word with an ominous tone. "What did you say?"

Calling upon all the courage she'd once possessed, Susanna raised her voice to an authoritative tone. "I will not marry Algernon."

Aunt Uriana's fingers twitched as if wishing to grab a switch and whip Susanna as she had those first explosive weeks after she became the new mistress of the manor. It hadn't taken long for Susanna to learn to bow—at least outwardly—to her aunt's will.

Undiluted poison came out of Aunt Uriana's voice. "You will do as I say or I will throw you out." She let out a mocking half-laugh. "You would have to work to support yourself." Her half laugh turned to a snigger. "Perhaps the wild dogs will make a meal of you."

Susanna ignored that last dart as she considered her options. Though quailing at the thought of working among strangers, seven years of practice helped Susanna appear poised. "I will find a position and support myself. I could be a governess or a lady's companion."

"Ha! As if anyone would want you! You wouldn't last one day."

Spreading open her hands, Susanna sifted through possible solutions. "I could—"

"Stop this foolish show of rebellion. We've already signed the settlement papers. The banns will be posted for the obligatory three Sundays, and then Algernon will come take you away." Aunt Uriana narrowed her eyes. "Must I lock you in your bedchamber until your wedding day?"

Susanna pressed a hand to her head. In reality, securing a position could take time, and she had precious little of that. Perhaps a show of compliance would be in order until she thought of a plan. Anger and panic boiled within her.

Still, she bowed her head and slumped her shoulders to appear the picture of servile obedience. "That will not be necessary, Aunt. You are right. I am ill-prepared to earn my own living. I will do as you wish."

The new parlor maid, Martha, entered carrying her cleaning rags. She drew up short, cast a panicked glance at Aunt Uriana and an apologetic one at Susanna. Silently, she curtsied and slipped out.

Aunt gave no indication she noticed the maid. "That's better. For your ill-mannered display, you are to go immediately to your bedchamber and remain there until I summon you...perhaps tomorrow. Perhaps longer. No tray will come to you. Now go."

Going without meals was a frequent enough occurrence, so Susanna voiced no complaint—such show of spine would only add to her sentence. Head still bowed, Susanna curtsied and left the morning room.

Oh, heaven help her, what was she to do now? Marrying Algernon was unthinkable. She'd rather starve to death locked in her bedchamber.

As she crossed the great hall, the black and white checkered tile reminded her of the private joke she and Papa had shared that someday they would use the floor as a human-sized chessboard. That day never came.

The distinct clattering of wheels and horse hooves on the cobbled drive reached her ears. She paused at the windows facing the front drive. The fountain splashed merrily, heedless of human travail. Behind it, gardeners mowed the expansive lawn. Along the drive rode a fine black carriage with red wheels.

Susanna groaned out loud. Not him. Not now. The conveyance pulled up to a stop and Percy, the only son of her Aunt Uriana, stepped out. Susanna hurried toward the stairs leading to the second floor. If she were fast enough, she could avoid his company.

The door opened and the butler's voice greeted the caller. Susanna quickened her pace but only made it up the first few steps.

"Ah, Susanna, there you are. I had hoped to see you." Percy's voice boomed through the great hall.

Susanna considered pretending she hadn't heard. They already thought her stupid and ugly and backwards; adding deafness to her list of faults would not hurt. However, she risked her overly-friendly cousin coming up the stairs after her, and that she could not abide.

Turning, she folded her hands and said formally, "Good morning, Cousin."

"Now, now. What's all this formality? After all, we are family." Percy smile sent a shiver slithering down her spine. "Come, come. Give me a proper greeting."

She descended the stairs as regally as she knew how. On the bottom step, she curtsied.

He chuckled. "That is not what I had in mind." His gaze lowered slowly down her body.

She backed up a step while cold chills raced down her arms. Trying to appear calm, she stared back at him boldly. With fair hair and skin, and patrician features, he might have been considered handsome by ladies, but Susanna had never found him appealing. His lips were too thick, his chin too soft, his stare bordering on improper.

"Ah, Percy, have you heard?" Aunt Uriana stood in the doorway of her morning room. "Algernon is going to marry Susanna."

"Is he now?" Percy lifted his brows. "Is this your desire, my little cousin?" His stare intensified.

Her aunt spared her from answering. "Of course. She is nearly twenty and has no other prospects. She'd be very foolish to turn him down." A pointed glance came Susanna's way. "Now, Percy dear, come and let's have a coze." She turned and went back inside her parlor.

Percy eyed her. Under his breath, he said, "I do

not believe you are happy about this union with Algernon, little Susie."

Susanna looked away. "Not...terribly so, but as Aunt Uriana said, I have no prospects."

Percy looked her over again as if examining a horse he considered buying. "I might be persuaded to help. With the right clothes and more attention to your hair, you might turn out well enough. I can take you away. Keep you in a quaint little cottage. Give you *cart blanche.*"

She stared. Did he mean what she thought? "But you are already married."

He laughed, a mocking sound. "No, sweet little Susie. I would not be your husband—I'd be your protector."

Her mouth dropped open. "You're asking me to be your...." She lowered her voice, "your *mistress?*"

"You would lack for nothing—a cottage all your own with servants, and fine clothes. I am much more generous with my mistresses than my mother is with poor relations." A slow, sensual smile twisted his thick lips. "Of course, I'd want a sampling of your sweetness before I make my true offer."

He seized her by both elbows and dragged her to him. A heartbeat before his mouth touched hers, her composure splintered. She kicked his shin. He arched back in surprise and released her.

"Never!" She whirled around and raced upstairs as if the devil were in pursuit.

He shouted a vulgar name but no pounding of footsteps came after her. With her heart hammering and sobs filling her lungs, she raced to her bedchamber, slammed the door and turned the lock. Of course, that might not keep him out. At ten years her senior, Percy still had the vitality of a young man.

Aunt Uriana had locked her in enough times that she knew her door could be unlocked from the other side. She must barricade herself in until he left. With what? Except for her bed and dressing table, both too heavy to move, only a small wooden stool remained in her bedchamber, and that would be too light to stop an intruder.

The dressing table remained her best option. She pushed and pushed and pushed, and finally moved it in front of the door. A really determined man, or an angry one, could probably still get in. At least this might slow him down enough for her to get away. She'd jump out the window if necessary.

She sank down on the window seat. What to do? She must leave before Percy pressed his suit, and before Algernon came to take her to the parson's noose. If she refused to marry Algernon, her aunt would starve her into submission. If she pretended to agree, and then refused at the altar, who knew what her aunt would do.

A scratch at the door caught her attention. Oh, no. Had Percy returned? Fear leaped into her throat. "Who is it?" she squeaked.

"It's Martha, miss," came the voice of the parlor maid. "I...forgive me, I know it's not my place but..." The maid paused. "May I come in?"

Susanna let out her breath. Safe, at the moment. To let the girl in, she must move the dressing table. "One moment." With much heaving, Susanna pushed the dressing table away enough to open the door. "Come in, Martha."

The maid stood in the doorway holding a small tray. She cast a curious glance at the dresser through wide gray eyes but returned her gaze to Susanna. In a low voice, she said, "In the missus' parlor, I wasn't listening, really I wasn't. But...I couldn't help but hear..." she bit her lip. "It's not really my place...."

Susanna gestured to her. "Come in, Martha. What is it? You can tell me."

The maid entered and waited until after Susanna had closed the door behind her. "I overheard the missus telling you that you weren't to come out of your bedchamber today—not even for meals—and I noticed you weren't at breakfast so...I brought you a bowl of fresh berries and a scone and cup of tea."

Susanna smiled. "Martha, you are a dear!"

Martha set down the tray. As Susanna sat on the

stool and devoured the food, Martha gestured to the new location of the dressing table. "Forgive me for asking, miss, but are you moving the furniture? Might I be of some assistance?"

Susanna swallowed. Confiding in one's servants really was not done, but the need to unburden herself became so great that she could hardly bear it another moment.

"My aunt is trying to force me to marry her nephew, Algernon, and my cousin Percy apparently desires me for his mistress."

"Oh, miss." Martha's eyes grew as round as the rim of Susanna's tea cup.

She'd rather marry an odious monster like Algernon than live as a fallen woman. "I moved the table in front of the door lest he decided to renew his proposition more...forcefully."

Martha glanced at the door as if fearing an army would storm the room.

Susanna finished off her scone. "I've endured seven years of abuse and now this. I cannot bear it any longer. The banns will be read Sunday next. If I had anywhere to go—other than to a life of scandal and sin—or any means to support myself, I'd leave now—today—but..." She shook her head.

"Could you? Support yourself, I mean?" asked the maid in uncharacteristic boldness. She clapped her hand over her mouth. "Forgive me, miss. It's not my place to ask impertinent questions." Shoulders slumping, she edged toward the door.

"It's quite all right, Martha; I would appreciate if you'd speak to me as you would a friend." Susanna gave the maid a sad smile. If she could discuss her thoughts with another person, she might happen upon a solution. "I have no one with whom I might discuss ideas. Please, won't you stay a moment? Please?"

She probably sounded like a desperate child. Truthfully, she *was* desperate, and frightfully low on options.

She gestured to the bed. "You may sit."

"If that pleases you, miss." Martha sat stiffly at the edge of the bed seat.

"I do not know what kind of position I could possibly obtain. Will you help me think of something?"

The maid adjusted her frilled cap. "I will help you all I can, miss."

"I'm afraid to venture out into the world. Leaving one's home and family simply isn't done. I have nowhere to go—my aunt cut off my friends years ago. And I have no living family besides my aunt and uncle. But I cannot bear this any longer. I must leave. I *must*."

Martha's eyes were full of sympathy. "I don't understand how they can treat you so poorly. I don't blame you for wishing to leave."

Susanna almost touched the maid but that would probably frighten her away. She settled for a friendly smile. "I thank you for your words. I feel rather naughty for even considering such a thing."

Martha smiled timidly.

"Tell me, Martha," Susanna said. "What can I do? What kinds of positions do young ladies obtain?"

Martha's brow wrinkled in thought. "A governess, perhaps?"

Susanna nodded. "I'd considered that. I read extensively, and speak French. But my aunt dismissed my governess when I was thirteen so I never received further education in history, or painting, or many other subjects a governess must know. I'm not sure I am educated enough." She finished the berries and sipped her tea.

Martha tapped her fingers together. "A lady's companion?"

"Yes, I'd thought of that as well. In truth, I do not know if I'm as well schooled as a lady's companion would need to be—if I understand the rules of etiquette. I have spent very little time outside my home."

"Perhaps a nursemaid."

14

Susanna let out a happy sigh and hope dared to rise up inside her. "I do love children."

"You'd need references," Martha said.

"Oh, dear." Her hope collapsed. "I have no such thing." Susanna put a hand to her head. Surely she was not doomed to marry Algernon. There had to be solution. She just needed to think of it.

"If I may be so bold; what skills do you have?" Martha asked.

Thoughtfully, Susanna took another sip of tea. "Skills? Very little, I'm afraid. Playing the harp is my only proficiency. Uncle always enjoys my harp music. It was at his pleasure I'd been allowed to continue taking lessons until two years ago."

Her uncle. She could appeal to him. He'd never been cruel to her, merely indifferent except when it came to music. He'd always provided a steady stream of new pieces for her to learn and play. Perhaps he might help.

She disregarded that thought. The few times she'd sought his aid, he'd turned her away, saying she ought to obey her aunt. Uncle either had no interest in Susanna beyond her music or he was so henpecked by his wife that he'd developed a habit of bowing to her every whim.

After finishing her tea, Susanna sank back down on her window seat. What might she do?

15

Martha fixed a focused stare on her. "Do you play the harp well enough to secure a position as teacher or perhaps as a musician?"

Susanna went still. "Work as a professional harpist? I have no idea."

"I don't have a trained ear, miss, but it seems to me that you have real skills, and you've been at it for years, haven't you?"

Susanna stood and paced. "I've been playing for many years. My last teacher declared me as talented and skilled as any harpist of his acquaintance and that there was nothing further he could teach me."

Since then, she played for her own enjoyment—the perfect escape from her present world into a magical world of music where no one reminded her she was backward or dull or ugly or stupid. Music had become her own private sanctuary.

She mused. "But to play professionally? Most professional musicians are men. I don't know if anyone would even give me a chance."

Martha's large brown eyes shone. "I went to the opera once and sat in the penny section. I did notice a few women in the orchestra. The opera houses employ musicians. So do some gardens such as Vauxhall. Why, the possibilities are endless. The London Season begins in a few weeks—right after Easter."

It sounded like a viable option. Oh, if she could do it, sharing her passion for music with others filled her with exhilaration. Still her confidence wavered. What if she wasn't good enough? Playing in a drawing room was one thing; playing as a professional was an entirely different matter.

Martha touched her hand. "The other musicians will recognize you as a member of the gentry and may not welcome you into their circles."

Susanna grappled with the information. Martha's words made sense. From what little she knew of the world, those who were raised as a lady but worked amid the working class were often outcasts no matter where they went. A governess was almost always shunned by servants, yet not treated like members of the family or guests by employers; she existed in a world in between worlds.

Did such a fate await Susanna in London?

More importantly, could she do this? What would people think of her? Would she face the same scrutiny as she did from her aunt? She couldn't bear it if someone were to criticize the one thing left that she loved so dearly. What if she weren't good enough?

She folded her arms and leaned over, "If I go, I may not find a position and then what would I do? If I find a position, I may not belong anywhere."

Gravely Martha said, "Also, I feel I must warn you

that professional musicians and actors are highly competitive. Jealousy is very strong. Some understudies have poisoned stars in order to take their place."

Perfect. She might not get a position either because of her gender or her lack of talent. If she did, she might be poisoned by another musician. Could it get any more uncertain and dangerous?

Susanna weighed her choices. "But staying with my aunt...that would be worse. I'd be forced to marry Algernon or continue to fend off Percy." She shook her head. "At least in London, I have a chance."

Martha nodded. "From what I understand, theatrical productions and operas always have premiers early in the Season. If you are to obtain a position with one of them before the Season begins, you may need to hurry."

Susanna's thoughts raced. "Then I must audition now or all the positions will be filled."

Yes, Susanna would leave. Now—before the banns were posted and before Percy renewed his offer more forcefully. More importantly, she'd leave before she lost her chances at making a living as a musician. London beckoned to her, promising a brighter future than any she'd imaged in years. Even if it meant isolation, she must take this chance. After all, a great deal of her life had been spent in solitude since her aunt and uncle became her guardians. Whether she could get a position before she starved was another matter. She was willing to take the risk.

Chapter Two

Excitement bubbled up inside Susanna at the possibilities that lay before her. "Oh, Martha, I do want to go to London to find work as a harpist. How would I get there?"

How *would* she get there? Susanna froze. She must travel alone, unprotected, and in the company of strangers. Still, remaining here seemed infinitely worse.

Martha frowned. "It doesn't seem right, a gently bred lady like yourself traveling all alone."

"Other people manage somehow," Susanna said, trying to be brave.

The maid-turned-confident paused. "That's true. I came here from London on the mail coach. It took three days. It is an uncomfortable way to travel because it only stops to change horses and drivers. That's when we stretched our legs and bought food at the posting inns. I didn't have to worry about paying for a bedchamber. But I'm used to being on my own."

Susanna considered. "I know where the nearest posting inn is. But once I reach London, I wouldn't know where to begin. I don't know all the theatres, nor how to go about getting a position, nor even where I'd stay." The unknowns all loomed before her like an endlessly high wall.

"I can't help you with getting a position, but I know the theatres." Martha started counting off on her fingers. "There's the King's Theatre, Covent Garden, Drury Lane, Lyceum...."

Susanna smiled at the sweet maid. What a dear she was for trying to help her! "I can see I should have spoken to you sooner."

Martha added, "I still can't like the idea of you traveling all the way to London alone, miss, but I admire your courage."

Courage or desperation? Either way, the more Susanna thought of it, the more determined she was to flee. Fear and excitement and anticipation tugged at her from every side, creating nervous anticipation. She'd never felt so terrified. Or so alive.

Martha helped her plan her route, told her where to exit the mail coach upon reaching London, and drew her a rough map of various theatres and opera houses.

"I only wish I could help you with a place to stay," Martha said. "I have no family and I doubt the missus at my former position would be of a mind to help; she wasn't exactly charitable by nature. You might try Mrs. Griffin's boarding house in St. James's Place. I hear she's respectable."

Susanna smiled. "Mrs. Griffin. I'll remember."

Excited that she had a better idea of what to do now, she and Martha went through Susanna's clothes, choosing her best ones to sell. Martha suggested Susanna dressed as a poor servant girl to help aid her anonymity, but after viewing Susanna's clothing, Martha clucked her tongue, shook her head, and declared her clothing shameless for the daughter of a gentleman, but sufficient for her new life.

Susanna glanced at the clock. "You'd best get back to your duties before you're missed. If anyone questions you about my disappearance, you don't know anything about where I went or when I left."

"I understand, miss." Martha nodded eagerly.

"Thank you." Impulsively, Susanna hugged Martha.

Martha hugged her back. "I hope you find what you need." She backed up, curtsied, and slipped out.

After Martha left, Susanna spent the remainder of the day scouring her bedchamber for anything which would be of value in a pawn shop, but only came up with her mother's wedding ring. She put it on her finger and admired it. The gold and sapphire ring glittered, fitting as if it had been made for her. It had been so lovely on her mother's graceful hand. Susanna hugged it. Could she part with such a cherished possession?

If it meant her only means of freedom, then yes—not easily, but she could. Mama would understand. Heavy of heart, but resolute, Susanna grabbed her pins and her best clothes, piling everything onto her bed.

Her parents' miniature sat on her dressing table, their smiling faces reminding her of a time when she was loved. She used to dream of being as beautiful as her mother—they shared the same abundant dark hair, but Mama's complexion had possessed an inner glow, and her eyes, the color of forget-me-nots, sparkled with laughter. Susanna was a colorless shadow of her mother. No wonder the only two men who expressed desire for her wanted her for all the wrong reasons. Honestly, it was a wonder they had any interest in her at all.

Martha returned with a threadbare portmanteau that smelled faintly of mothballs. "I found this up in the attic, miss. And I brought you some more food from the kitchen." She held out a small cloth bundle. "Cheese and bread and two apples. I took them when the cook wasn't looking. It won't last you the entire journey, but it will give you a start."

When was the last time someone had shown such kindness? If their situation had been different, she and Martha might have been fast friends. "Martha, what would I do without you?"

The maid hesitated, her smile turning sad. "I wish I had more to give you."

"You've done so much already. Thank you."

"Good luck, miss."

Alone again, Susanna wrapped the miniature in a chemise, she tucked it into the portmanteau. Finally, she packed the letters from her brother, Richard, the only thing she had of him. On top of the stack bound with ribbon lay the letter from the Admiralty informing her of his death and another from his captain expressing his condolences.

A storm of sorrow and regret, and even anger blew over her. If only Richard had come home sooner, he would be alive, they would have each other, and Susanna would never have had to endure years of her aunt's abuse. She pictured his lopsided smile, recalled the pure joy in his laugh, remembered the way he used to tug on her hair and call her Susie Bug. He'd taught her to swim. He'd even challenged her to walk into a dark room when she was afraid. If he could speak to her from the grave, he would urge her to take this chance in London.

She stared at the portmanteau. She was doing this. She was really going to leave her childhood home—the only home she'd ever known. More importantly, she would leave Aunt Uriana's dominion and have the freedom to pursue her own course, perhaps even choose her own husband—provided any man would want someone like her. It seemed a bit unreal—like a dream.

To pass the time until she could leave undetected, she curled up in the window seat and pulled out one of her Sweet Memories, a term her mother used to describe those times to cherish and to recall whenever she needed to cheer herself. Today, Susanna immersed herself in memories of sitting in this very window seat, holding a china doll and listening to her mother read to her from a book of Perrault's Fairy Tales. She had adored the story of the Sleeping Beauty, whose brave prince saved her and her kingdom from an enchantment, and of Cinderella, who had risen from difficult circumstances to marry a charming prince. Most of all, she had loved resting her head on Mama's lap, listening to her lovely contralto voice paint vivid pictures with her words of magic and adventure and love.

"Adventure and love," she repeated with a sigh. Perhaps London offered those as well. She let out a scoff. She'd settle for honest work and a place to sleep.

Tonight she'd walk to the village, sell what she could, and catch the mail coach. Once she reached London, she'd present herself to every theatre and opera house in London. Surely someone would need a harpist of her skill, or would know of someone who would. Her plan depended on a bit of luck and not a few prayers, but new confidence filled her.

The very singular day faded into night. Still Susanna waited. Outside, owls hooted and frogs sang in a rough chorus as the house sank into utter stillness. Hours later, the hall clock chimed two o'clock in the morning. Finally, Susanna donned her only bonnet, coat, and gloves.

Her pulse throbbed. With shaking fingers, from both excitement and trepidation, Susanna unlocked the door and opened it. The hinges squeaked. She held her breath. Moments passed. No sound indicated anyone had heard.

This was mad. What was she thinking? She couldn't run away in the middle of the night. She would be entirely alone, and had only a few coins in her pocket. Even if she managed to reach London safely, she had no position and nowhere to sleep. Aunt and Uncle and their horrid son and nephew were her only relations. She had been cut off from friends for years—they had probably all forgotten her.

What choice did she have? Staying here to either marry Algernon or be ravished by Percy was unthinkable. Besides, if she reached London, she could go to the Admiralty and search for more information about Richard's death. Why she needed the details of his last few moments alive, she could not say, but not knowing had left a hollowness inside her.

She opened the door and stole out into the corridor with her few possessions, a prayer in her heart, and courage born of desperation.

Creeping through the house using the servants' stairs, she entertained the idea of taking something of value to aid in her flight. However, knowing her aunt would view that as theft, she refrained. Susanna stopped in the drawing room. Moonlight spilled in through sheer curtains at the windows, painting pale patterns on the floor and illuminating her harp.

She moved to the elegant stringed instrument and caressed the curves of its neck. Her friend. Her solace. Now, with a healthy serving of luck, it would be her means of obtaining independence. She couldn't bring the harp of course—it belonged to her uncle now, along with the estate. Leaving it behind sent a dart of pain through her heart. It had provided countless hours of escape from the misery of her life. It had absorbed her anger, her sorrow, her frustration, her loneliness. It always gave back peace and contentment. It had probably kept her alive. She ran her hand down the harp's soundboard, tracing the gilded vines and flowers. The knowledge and skill she had gained would remain with her.

She choked, "Good bye, my friend." One last time, she covered the instrument, gave it a final pat, and left the room. A piece of her heart remained behind.

Outside, she hurried along the trees lining the drive, using the shadows to conceal her in the event someone spotted her. A blazingly bright moon lit her path and a breeze cooled her perspiration-dampened hair. Her heart thumped. If she were caught, she would be locked in her bedchamber and lose her chance for escape. Fear kept her running as fast as she dared in the semi-darkness. A stitch in her side slowed her and her arms ached from carrying the portmanteau, but she kept moving, alternating between running and walking. If she had been any less familiar with her surroundings, she might have been afraid. Her imagination painted images of bandits lurking in every shadow. However, this area had been her home all her life.

As she reached the village, the eastern horizon shimmered silver, gilding clouds as they peeped out from behind distant mountains. Signs of life arose with the sun. A goose girl herded her charges, and the blacksmith's hammer rang out. Chickens clucked and a baby cried nearby as Susanna passed by shops and picked her way to the pawn shop next to the mercantile.

She pushed open the door and almost let out an audible sigh that she'd made it this far. "Mrs. Miller?" she called.

Footsteps and a swishing skirt announced the

owner's arrival. "May I help you?" With lively eyes peering out from underneath her white frilled cap, Mrs. Miller blinked at Susanna as if she didn't recognize her.

Indeed, they had not conversed much over the years since her parents' death but she remembered going with her mother when she visited tenants and villagers, sometimes bringing baskets of food even when it wasn't Boxing Day. Mrs. Miller had always received them warmly. Since then, Susanna had only glimpsed Mrs. Miller in church—on the days her aunt allowed her to attend.

Susanna smiled. "Good morning, Mrs. Miller. It's Susanna Dyer."

Mrs. Miller's eyes widened. "Well bless my soul, so it is. I haven't seen you around much—I heard you were poorly."

"Not as 'poorly' as my aunt and uncle would like you to believe. I have some things I need to sell." She showed the woman her clothes, pins, and the miniature. "I'm not interested in letting go of the portrait, of course, but I thought perhaps the frame would be of value?"

Mrs. Miller looked them all over. Under the woman's scrutiny, the articles Susanna had brought suddenly looked shabby and worthless. Kindly, the woman asked, "Why do you need money, Miss Susanna?"

"I need to buy passage on the mail coach."

Mrs. Miller studied her. "I see. Your aunt and uncle aren't treating you well, are they?"

Exhaustion and fear and uncertainty drained her composure. Tears pricked her eyes. She looked down to cover signs of her emotion. "Please, is any of this worth anything?"

"Is this your mother's wedding band?" Mrs. Miller picked up the gold and sapphire ring and held it into the light.

Tears escaped. Susanna hastily brushed them away and nodded. "It's all I have of hers—and this miniature."

"I think we can work out something."

"And please, if anyone asks, you haven't seen me. They can't know where I've gone."

Mrs. Miller patted her hand. "I understand, my dear. You have my silence."

Susanna left the shop with a lighter portmanteau and a few coins wrapped up in a handkerchief and tucked into her stays. A few hours later, Susanna sat atop a mail coach and offered a prayer that she would reach London safely, procure employment, and find a place to stay.

"And," she added to her whispered prayer, "if it isn't too much to ask, a guardian angel would be very helpful about now."

The coach bumped along and Susanna held on

for her life, not bothering to wipe away the tears she shed for leaving behind her mother's ring, her harp, her home, her village, and everything she had ever known. Eventually, she dried her tears and looked ahead. London, and all its possibilities awaited. If nothing else, she'd be safe from her horrid relations who wanted her for their own purposes. And maybe, just maybe, she would prove to herself and them that she was smart and capable. Or at the very least, worthwhile.

Chapter Three

If only every day were so fine, Christopher Anson could die a happy man. Eager as always for tonight's performance, Kit tucked his violin case under his arm and strolled along the sidewalk toward the now-familiar brick building graced with statues, arches, and a dome that made up the King's Theatre. Some musicians cited the thrill of playing for an audience, but Kit loved playing music for its own sake. Besides, performing for an audience meant the conductor wouldn't stop the orchestra and break up the flow of music nor the fluid beauty running into Kit's soul. Solos were all fine and well, but being part of a group created a magical blend he could not produce on his own.

As he approached the back of the King's Theatre toward the stage entrance, a small figure arose from its crouched position. Another urchin, no doubt. Without breaking stride, Kit reached into his pocket to toss the poor creature a coin.

"Excuse me, sir."

He halted. Such cultured tones did not belong to a street urchin. In fact, they sounded a great deal like the voice of a lady. He peered more closely at the form. A gray, threadbare woman's coat, and a decade-old straw bonnet engulfed a body about half his width and barely the height of his shoulder—and he was no giant. She gripped a bag resembling a sad excuse for a portmanteau. The form lifted her head and a large pair of eyes almost the color of the coat peered at him. A decidedly feminine, young face accompanied those eyes.

"Forgive me for my intrusion, sir, but are you a musician at this theatre?"

Almost speechless at the incongruity of her voice and appearance, he nodded. "I am."

She heaved a small breath of relief. "I am trying to see the conductor—to audition for the role of harpist—but the door guard refused me entrance. Please, can you help me get inside to speak with the conductor?"

He lifted his brow and looked her over more carefully. "You are a harpist?"

"Yes, sir. I have played for the past sixteen years."

"You don't look old enough to have been alive these past sixteen years."

"I began taking lessons when I was three. I am now nineteen—nearly twenty."

Nineteen? Much more grown up than she appeared. Her coat hung limply straight from the shoulders, giving no hint of a womanly figure. She must be half starved or sickly.

"I'm sorry, miss, but we already have an orchestra harpist." Of course, the current harpist, though skilled, played with very little emotion, notwithstanding that Kit suspected the man to be a bit unhinged. Kit gave her an apologetic smile. "Auditions are conducted weeks before each new production, and the musicians are selected by a panel of judges including the manager."

"Perhaps I could be a secondary harpist–like an understudy the singers have?"

"That's not up to me."

"Please, sir, can't you get me in to at least plead my case to the conductor? Surely he has some influence with the theatre manager or this panel of judges."

Her pleading eyes reminded him of a sad puppy. Kit was never cruel to puppies. "Very well, but Alex is a temperamental man; I cannot guarantee he'll even speak with you."

She let out her breath as if she had been holding it. "Oh, thank you so much. I don't mean to be a bother, but I am rather, er that is, I..." She glanced at him from underneath her lashes as if fearing his temper. "I really need the work."

Kit had been a hungry musician once, too. And something about her brave yet desperate plea touched his heart. "Follow me." He knocked on the door.

The door guard opened it and stuck his face out. "Oh, Mr. Anson, it's you."

"Good evening, Bert." Kit glanced over his shoulder at the ragged girl. "She's with me."

The door guard hesitated, clearly torn between rules and his desire to stay in Kit's good graces. "Er, as you wish, sir."

"My thanks." He retrieved a hot cross bun from his pocket and handed it to Bert. "They're fresh today."

Bert grinned. "Thankee, sir."

The harpist-waif kept close to Kit as he mounted the steps and entered the stage, dodging curtains, ropes, dancers warming up, vocalists running through trills, and the stage crew carrying pieces of the set. The *prima donna*, painted like a character from a bygone era, whined about the fit of her costume, and one of the dancers silently wrapped her bleeding foot in a strip of cloth before pulling on her ballet slipper. Kit spared a thought for the dancer, but such occurrence was so common that everyone looked at him as if he had grown a second head when he offered aid.

At the top of the stairs leading to the orchestra pit, he glanced at the opulent auditorium, unceasingly awed by the fresco-painted, domed ceiling, the three levels of seating, and private boxes on each side of the stage. Invigorated by the sight, Kit descended into the orchestra pit with his little shadow trailing him. He glanced back at the girl who looked around her with wide eyes.

"Now?" thundered the conductor, Alex. "He's just now telling me this?"

A young stagehand shrugged and trotted up the stairs to the stage.

The conductor tugged on his hair. "I can't believe this!"

"What's amiss, Alex?" Kit asked, while the rest of the orchestra ignored his outburst.

Alex Abbiati, one of the most brilliant young conductors of the decade, turned to him, his brown skin reddening and his coal-black eyes flashing. "The harpist injured his hand today and cannot play." He let out a groan. "I knew we should have hired a secondary harpist. This one is so temperamental and...odd...that I had a feeling we ought to have someone ready in the wings."

Kit blinked. A harpist appears begging for work the same time their orchestra harpist is injured and cannot play? What were the chances of that? Perhaps fate was on this girl's side. Or an angel watched over her.

Alex paced back and forth, tugging on his black hair until it stood on end in all directions as if he had been out in an electric storm. "I suppose we'll have to change your duet in the second act from harp and violin to pianoforte and violin. I'll have to send word to Marcus. He's the only one I know who can sight read well enough to perform without rehearsal."

"Perhaps we have another option." Kit glanced over his shoulder at the waif-who-would-be-harpist shadowing him, but she had already stepped around him.

With all the poise of a duchess, she approached Alex and sank into a curtsy fit for the queen's drawing room. "Sir, if I may; I am an excellent sight-reader. If you'd be so kind as to allow me to audition, I believe you will agree I am a suitable replacement."

Alex's mouth opened in surprise. "You play the pianoforte?"

"No, sir, I am a harpist."

Alex took a quick measure of her, his passionate Italian features taking on a speculative edge. "I do not have time for little girls with illusions of grandeur. Leave at once!"

Unimpressed with his temper, she remained composed. "I assure you sir, I am very accomplished. My last master was Phillip Schlomovitz and I studied under him for four years."

Her declaration took him aback. "Schlomovitz, you say?"

"Yes, sir," she said with quiet firmness. "If you

give me a copy of the score, I am confident I will prove myself adequate."

Still, Alex hesitated.

The waif's quiet courage and determination, not to mention her outward serenity against an angry man twice her size won Kit's admiration. Besides, Kit remembered all too well what it was like to beg for a chance to prove himself as a musician.

"Give her a chance, Alex," Kit said. "You gave me one. With curtain half an hour away, we've little to lose."

Alex threw up his hands. "Oh, very well." He gestured to the resident harp at the back of the orchestra pit behind the second violin section. "Impress me."

The girl's smile lit up her face, turning her plainness into a thing of, well, perhaps not beauty, but at least less bland. She picked her way through the string section to the harp. The girl set down her portmanteau and removed her coat revealing a thin figure and a faded, threadbare gown that a servant would have been embarrassed to wear. Discarding her hat displayed a thick head of dark hair twisted into a knot trying to pass for a hairstyle his sister called a chignon. Hairpins, he supposed, were an expense she could not afford. She removed the harp cover with a practiced tug and adeptly tuned the instrument with long, slender fingers.

Kit joined her in the back of the orchestra pit. After rosining his bow and tuning his violin to her harp, he waited for her to warm up with a series of scales and arpeggios. A few moments later, he pointed to a spot in her music. "Alex wants to hear you play our duet in the second act."

She fixed large eyes on him. "*Our* duet?"

"It's for harp and violin, and I'm the principal violinist," he explained.

She nodded, swallowed, and took a deep breath. "Whenever you are ready, sir."

"I'm ready."

She wiped her hands on her skirts, and moved the pedals to put the harp into the correct key. Alex folded his arms, determined not to be impressed. The girl placed her fingers on the strings. And played.

Kit was so thunderstruck by the skill and beauty issuing forth from the instrument that he barely remembered to come in at the right time. Quickly, he raised his violin to his chin, lifted his bow, and closed his eyes. They played together. All the world—all noise, other performers, the audience entering—all else faded away. Kit and his violin, and the girl with her harp, were the only creations in the universe. Together, they produced magic. His soul sang as loudly as his violin.

As the last notes of their duet faded away, Kit let out his breath and swallowed the knot in his throat.

Such beauty and passion. This little waif was a true musician. In all his five and twenty years, he had never heard her equal.

Kit lowered his violin and clutched his bow. Meeting her gaze, he smiled. "Brava."

Alex sniffed. "Humph, you'll do. Watch that key change—A natural."

Before he strode away, he glanced at Kit, and his approval revealed itself. Kit grinned. She had impressed Alex—no small feat.

Kit gave her a friendly smile. "Welcome aboard, Miss...?"

"Susanna Dyer."

He inclined his head in an abbreviated bow. "Kit Anson, at your service."

She stood and curtsied. "Thank you, Mr. Anson, for your assistance convincing him to allow me to audition."

He shrugged. "We had nothing to lose."

"You play magnificently." Shy admiration entered her eyes.

"As do you."

She frowned at the music. "He's right—it should have been A natural." She resumed her seat and played it correctly, although few would have noticed her minor error earlier. Then she flipped to the beginning of her music and began practicing. The

40

serenity in her expression, the concentration in her eyes, the graceful movement of her fingers captured his attention, as did the beauty she created as she played. Perhaps it was the lighting or her talent coloring Kit's perception of her, but Susanna Dyer appeared less a dingy, half-starved waif, and more a captivating young lady he might have been happy to meet during his former life.

Her fingers paused in their intricate dance with the strings, and she fixed her gaze on him. "Thank you again, Mr. Anson."

He grinned to cover his embarrassment that she had caught him staring. "You're welcome. By the way, we aren't so formal in the orchestra. My friends call me Kit."

His sister had begun calling him Kit when she was little, a name she called him even now that she was a wise married lady, so he had come to think of himself by that name. When he left home, he had begun introducing himself as Kit Anson. The name suited him better, anyway.

Susanna Dyer glanced at him, offered a strained smile, and returned her attention to the music, a clear dismissal, and without giving him permission to use her given name. He paused, his pride deflating a little. Women seldom treated him so dismissively. Perhaps he had gotten too accustomed to charming any woman he chose.

Still, he respected that she was a serious musician. Now that he thought of it, he found it refreshing to meet a lady not interested in flirting with him or trying to gain his favor for her own purposes. How unlike ladies in the ballrooms he once frequented before his self-imposed banishment.

Kit returned to his seat in the front and trained his ears on the harp music floating from the back of the pit while he prepared for performance.

On stage, all the usual drama and a few mistakes of a theatrical production proceeded. Kit reveled in it all, especially the music, which was as nearly perfect as he'd ever heard, thrilled to be a part of a greater whole creating beauty and power. As the final curtain fell and applause rose and died away, Kit stood, nodded to his stand partner who was probably plotting to usurp Kit, shook hands with Alex, and glanced back at the harpist.

She sat like a ragged little urchin behind a harp too big for her small frame with her face glowing in after-performance euphoria. He caught her gaze and smiled. She beamed. Under the force of her stunning smile, he nearly dropped his bow. By Jove, she was pretty when she smiled.

He lost sight of the harpist in the chaos that always came after the curtain fell. As he made his way to the harp to speak with her, he spotted Alex in conversation with her. She nodded, then smiled brilliantly. Kit blinked. Yes, indeed, very pretty when she smiled. Or perhaps part of the beauty came from that portion of her soul she bared when she played.

Alex nodded and stepped back. As he passed Kit, he said, "I have a few notes for you, as well."

Kit moved to the harpist as she covered her instrument. "Miss Susanna, you are heaven-sent."

Practically glowing, she let out a half laugh. "Believe me, this was an answer to my prayers." Her smile faltered. "Not that I wish any harm on the other harpist, but..."

He chuckled. "I know what you mean."

"I thank you for your assistance." She nodded in Alex's direction. "The conductor asked me to return tomorrow night."

"I'm glad to hear it."

She let out a happy sigh, her eyes sparkling like a brook in the sunshine. "Well, good night." She donned her shapeless, ugly coat. "I suppose I shall see you tomorrow evening."

She would be back tomorrow. The thought shouldn't thrill him the way it did. He had no interest in romantic entanglements, especially with a ragged little urchin who played like an angel.

He almost let out a sigh as happy as hers. "Good night."

Perhaps the manager would offer her a permanent position as secondary harpist. A pity he couldn't make her the principal—she certainly deserved it. And she was a bright spot where the regular harpist was such a blight in the beauty of the music. Kit packed his violin and conferred with Alex. By the time they finished, the orchestra pit had emptied. Kit exited the theatre. The statues gracing the top of the three-level building seemed to bid him farewell. Kit shook his head at the fanciful notion. With visions of a hot meal awaiting him making his mouth water he crossed the street. A now-familiar form stood under a streetlamp, barely visible in the growing fog. The little harpist. She glanced up and down the street indecisively.

"Are you lost, Miss Susanna?" he called out.

Her head snapped toward him but she didn't censure him for using her given name. "Oh, Mr. Anson. Good evening." She curtsied and turned away.

She meant it as a farewell, but he stopped next to her. "Do you require assistance?"

She let out a little nervous laugh. "No, I just, er...goodnight." She made a vague gesture and started walking as if she had chosen a direction at random.

He cocked his head. "Are you truly lost or do you have nowhere to stay?"

She folded in even tighter. "I arrived just today so I don't know my way around just yet."

"From where?"

After a brief hesitation, she replied, "The Thames Valley."

"And you arrived with no arrangements of a place to sleep?"

"I didn't say I had no place to sleep; I said I just arrived and I am not yet familiar with London so I am easily turned around." She drew herself up primly. "Good night."

Questions about her flitted through his mind—why a gently bred lady had come to London looking like a half-starved orphan and desperate for work. That she had somehow fallen on hard times, he did not doubt. Either she had no family or she had run away. How long had she been alone?

He deliberated what, if anything, he should do about her. "Wait."

She paused, shifted her hold on her bag, and glanced back.

He tucked his violin under his arm. "I am in the habit of eating very little before a performance, so I dine afterward. I'd be pleased if you'd join me—I know a little pub nearby that serves excellent food."

"Thank you, but I must decline. Enjoy your dinner." She curtsied like a lady in a ballroom and strode the opposite direction from where she had headed moments ago, head high, walking with firm, decisive steps.

He paused, oddly disappointed that she had dismissed him yet again. And really, a young girl shouldn't be traipsing around London alone.

He trotted to catch up with her but she disappeared into the fog. "Susanna? Miss Dyer?"

No answer.

"Miss Dyer!"

Still nothing.

A rumble in his stomach prodded him again. Still, he could not easily dismiss her. He would never let his sister walk the streets alone, especially not at night. He made a circle, retracing his steps several times, but the fog thickened, devouring everything within a few feet of his face. Finally, he conceded defeat. Susanna seemed resourceful and confident. Surely she would be well.

Hunger urged him onward to his destination. He whistled as he strode down the cobbled streets but glanced back twice to look for her. Still no sign of the surprising girl.

Before long, the sign for the Silver Duck pub swung back and forth on creaking hinges, calling a friendly greeting. Kit stepped in and took his usual seat. The regular diners had all gone home. A few men hunched together, murmuring and drinking from tankards.

"Evenin' Kit," called the owner as he wiped the bar. "'ow was yer performance?"

Kit grinned. "Good evening, Ol' Joe. A few mishaps but nothing of which the audience would have been aware." Including a little drama involving the orchestra harpist and a timely newcomer.

The owner nodded. "I presume yer 'ungry."

Kit grinned. "You are a mind-reader."

Joe disappeared into the kitchen and reappeared a few minutes later with a bowl of lamb stew in one hand and a half a loaf of bread on a tin plate in the other.

"Yer probably me last one tonight, so finish off this 'ere bread, will ya?" Joe set the food on the table and stood wiping his hands.

"You're too good to me, Ol' Joe." Kit tucked into his meal, ignoring Joe's sniggering about his "high falutin' table manners." As he ate, he thought again of the new little harpist. He relived the glory of playing the duet with her. Having another opportunity to recreate that experience with her left him almost giddy. Tomorrow night wouldn't come soon enough.

Kit finished his food with a satisfied sigh. He tossed a coin on his way out. "My thanks, Ol' Joe."

Ol' Joe caught it and held it up, continuing their ritual. "You paid too much, you know."

"That's for keeping it hot and ready for me." Kit put on his hat and left the pub with a full belly and thoughts of his warm bed waiting for him. Upon reaching his bachelor's rooms, a message awaited him.

He held the letter, staring at Mother's familiar handwriting on the outside. Why was it so hard to open and read it? He had no quarrel with her. He had even had dinner with her on occasion each time she came to London—after ensuring his father would not be in attendance, that is. Messages from home always reopened old wounds, old arguments. Still, Kit was no coward. He tore the seal and opened the letter.

My dearest son,

We've come to London early for the Season. Your father has business and I miss you terribly. I know you're still proving you are your own man and probably enjoying your independence, but you've been gone far longer than I thought you would, and I had really hoped you would pay me a call more often. Now that we are in town, do join me for breakfast tomorrow. I'll have Cook make extra eggs. I brought hothouse strawberries with me from home.

I remain

Your loving mother

He smiled. Breakfast with his mother sounded pleasant. She had certainly brought the right bait—strawberries. He would make a point of arriving late enough to give his father an opportunity to have absented himself or Kit might be tempted to do something he would later regret.

Chapter Four

A bang uncomfortably nearby awakened Susanna from a fitful sleep. She peered around the wooden crates that had made up her temporary home. Exhaustion from a nearly sleepless night weighed her limbs and left her eyes hot and gritty. Every time she had nodded off, lulled to sleep with a Sweet Memory, a strange sound had roused her, and the terror that some unsavory character bent on bringing harm to her had prevented a deep sleep—not to mention the cold damp, the horrific smells, and her uncomfortable position crouched against a building.

If only the boarding house Martha had recommended had been willing to take her in. Without a letter of introduction and enough money to pay for a week in advance, none of those she tried would have her. If she had known she would be sleeping in the streets, she might never have left home for London.

No, that wasn't true. Playing in a symphony orchestra for an opera had exceeded her imagination—not to mention that duet she played with the stunning, dark-haired Kit Anson...oh my! She thought she had been transported to heaven. What a glorious, joyful union that had been. Surely kissing couldn't be more wondrous than that experience—not that she had thought of kissing when she had gazed at Kit's handsome face or his expressive mouth. Not at all. And that smile he'd sent her, the approval shining in his brown eyes, had been sublime.

Nearby, a ragged figure dug through a pile of refuse, tossing unwanted items into the alley and pocketing others. Susanna stood, cramped muscles protesting after having spent hours curled in a ball. Her numb feet refused to move and sharp tingles raced down her legs. She tried to lick her lips but her tongue stuck to the roof of her mouth. If only she could find a cup of water! After a moment, the feeling returned in her feet and the pain left her legs. Moving quietly so as not to alert the scavenger to her presence, she gripped her portmanteau and crept out of her hiding spot. She skulked down the alley to the edge of the avenue. So early in the morning, little traffic traversed the streets so she strode unimpeded down a street called Haymarket to the imposing King's Theatre.

Outside the stage door, she paused to smooth her hair. How she missed her bed, a basin of clean water, and most of all—food. Even sporadic meals were better than none. Still, she had no regrets about leaving. Here in London she was free—free from her aunt's constant fault-finding, free from Cousin Percy's improper advances, and free from marriage to a toad. A few more days of hunger was a small price to pay for such a great prize. And the conductor, Alex, had told her she was to come back tonight—perhaps all week, depending on the extent of the other harpist's injury. The thrill of seeing Kit again, of playing music with him, filled her with such delight that the money she would earn seemed secondary. Almost. Having a safe place to lay her head, and food to eat would be sublime.

She reached the huge brick structure and went to the stage door. She knocked smartly. And waited. She knocked louder. Nothing. She must be too early. It was probably just as well. She might have difficulty speaking with her mouth and throat so dry. Perhaps she could find water somewhere. Regardless, she appeared to have time on her hands. She sighed and hefted her portmanteau. After stopping at an outhouse behind a haberdashery, she wandered down the street, gazing into shop windows, and trying not to stare at the breads displayed in the bakery.

Even with Susanna eating as little as possible, the food Martha had provided had only lasted three days. The money from Mrs. Miller's pawn shop paid for her mail coach ride and two meals. The journey had taken longer than expected, first due to bad weather and then a broken wheel. Hence, Susanna had eaten nothing during her last two days of travel. Since her arrival in London yesterday, she'd had no other means of feeding herself.

No matter. She had employment now, at least for a few days. After that, she could ask for a letter of introduction to gain access to other orchestras. Perhaps now that she had a position, however temporary, she could appeal to one of the boarding houses again.

A pub with the whimsical name of the Silver Duck caught her attention. Then another sound came—running water. She followed the sound down a narrow alley similar to the one where she had spent the night. Presently, she came to a woman filling two buckets of water from a pump. Susanna hung back, fearful of the other's reaction.

As the woman hefted her buckets, Susanna's desperation overcame her fear. "Please, ma'am. May I have some water?"

The worker glanced at her and shrugged. "Suit yeself."

Susanna approached the pump and set down her bag where it would be out of the way. Gingerly, she lifted the handle as she had seen the woman do. Cool clear water shot out of the spigot. Susanna released the handle, cupped her hand and drank and drank, quenching her thirst and attempting to fill her empty stomach. After drinking all she could hold, she washed her hands and face and brushed her teeth. Then, after putting a little water on her hairbrush, she freed her hair from its knot, brushed it, and twisted it up again at the nape of her neck. How refreshing!

A girl about her own age emerged from the back door of another establishment. She approached, carrying two buckets.

Feeling more like a lady and less like gutter trash, Susanna nodded at the other girl. "Good morning."

The girl stared as if Susanna had spoken to her in a foreign language, moved to the pump, and filled her buckets. Susanna picked up her portmanteau and returned to the King's Theatre.

This time, the grizzled guard opened the door and peered at her. "Eh?"

What had Kit called the guard? Bert, that was it. She smiled. "Good morning, Bert. I am here to speak with the manager, please."

Bert screwed up his face and looked her over as if he couldn't take her measure. She stood up straight and smiled with a confidence she didn't feel. Silently, she pled for him to comply.

"Who are ye?" he finally asked.

"I am Susanna Dyer, remember? I'm the replacement harpist who played last night for the resident harpist who injured his hand?"

He blinked.

"I came in with Kit Anson?" she prompted. His name revived memories of a pair of warm brown eyes and a face far too handsome for his own good—for *her* own good. He had been a joy to watch as he played, his eyes closed much of the time, his hands moving so gracefully as he played, his lean body swaying slightly. When he had spoken, his voice had been a smooth baritone that made her wonder if he sang as well as he played. He had not only behaved as a gentleman but had been uncommonly kind. She had found in Kit a perfect opposite of Algernon. Or Percy. Not only was he dark to their fair coloring, and handsome to their plainness, but the differences in their conduct set them as clear opposites.

"Ooooh, right. Now I remember ye." Bert opened the door wide enough to let her in, and looked in all directions as if he expected her to have brought a den of thieves.

She waited for him to finish locking the door before she spoke. "If you would be so kind as to point me in the direction of the manager's office."

"It's next t' the booth."

"And that is where?"

He grumbled something under his breath. "I'll take ye."

He led her through a dark maze of curtains,

54

ropes, and pieces of the set backstage, down a narrow passageway, and up a flight of stairs. Finally, he took her to a door between a row of chairs.

"That's it." He turned and left.

"Thank you, Bert."

He grunted without halting his steps.

Susanna raised her hand to knock, but the floor rocked beneath her feet and black spots appeared before her eyes. She grabbed onto the nearest chair as her knees buckled.

Breathe, breathe. She fought back the darkness. How long she sat gripping the chair and trying to stop the spinning she could not have guessed. Eventually, the world righted. She had best eat soon or she would not have the strength to perform. How embarrassing it would be to faint in the middle of the performance. They would probably throw her out without blinking an eye.

Leaving her portmanteau on a chair near the door, she drew a breath and knocked.

"Enter!" a man barked.

Inside, she found a middle-aged gentleman with a full head of gray hair and long, wide mutton chops. He poured over papers scattered on his desk and scribbled with a quill.

She clasped her hands together and waited. And waited. Finally, she said, "Excuse me, sir."

He gave a start as if he had forgotten she was there. "Who the devil are you?"

"Susanna Dyer, sir, your replacement harpist. The conductor said he would speak to you about me?"

"What?" he narrowed his eyes at her. "Oh, yes. What do you want? I'm a very busy man."

"I came to discuss the possibility of my remaining with the company on a more long-term basis."

He eyed her. "You can play tonight, but beyond that depends on how long the principal harpist is out. I have to discuss it with Alex and my business partners. Come back tomorrow."

Tomorrow?

"Sir, I had rather hoped that I could collect pay for last night's performance as well as dis—"

"All performers will be paid Friday next."

A whole week away? Panic sent a tremor down her spine.

"Sir, I am rather in need of funds at the moment—"

"I don't care what you need. I have an entire cast and crew to manage as well as the musicians. I cannot cater to one."

His habit of cutting her off battered her nerves but she kept her composure. "It is not my wish to cause you any inconvenience, sir, but—"

"Look." He took a breath in an obvious attempt

to control his temper. "Even if I were willing to pay you early, I don't keep money here for payroll. You will have to wait until next Friday. Good day." In a clear dismissal, he picked up his pen and resumed writing.

She refused to surrender so easily. "Sir, I am not asking for much—"

"I said good day."

"—just enough coin that I might buy a bit of bread."

He lifted his head.

"Please, sir. A shilling. Anything."

Either his heart softened or she looked particularly close to swooning. He heaved a long-suffering sigh and reached into his pocket. His mouth pursed as he retrieved a coin and tossed it to her. "That's all I have on my person."

She scrambled to catch it. A farthing. She hugged it. "Thank you, sir."

"It will come out of your pay."

"Of course, sir."

"Out." He picked up his pen, inspected the tip, and resumed writing.

"Thank you, sir. I'm very grateful to you for your kindness." She curtsied and left, closing the door behind her.

A farthing. She had no hope of it lasting an entire

week, but it would feed her today. Picking up her portmanteau as she passed by the chair, she retraced her steps. She cast a longing glance at the orchestra pit. Did she dare leave her portmanteau there? It would spare her having to carry it everywhere. Surely with Bert guarding the entrance it would be safe. But that bag contained everything she owned. No, she dare not risk it.

The door guard sat whittling by the light of a sputtering candle. He looked up at her approach.

"Thank you, Bert." She smiled.

He nodded, unlocked the door and let her out.

Susanna paused, unsure of which direction to take. She had seen a bakery and the pub where she had washed this morning, but had no idea where would be the most economical place to purchase food.

In the time that it took her to speak with the opera manager, the streets had filled with the working class carrying boxes and baskets, some pushing handcarts, others driving horse-drawn conveyances. Horse hooves clopped, wheels clattered over streets, vendors announced their wares, and friends called greetings. In the distance, a child wailed. Closer, men laughed. Scents of meat pies and bread mingled with flowers, horses, unwashed bodies, and the unique aroma of the Thames.

Susanna headed in the direction of the bakery

58

she had spotted earlier, too hungry to care if it had the best food or the most reasonable prices.

"Well, well, good day to you, Missy," a male voice said in such heavy Cockney that she had to mentally translate to decipher his meaning.

If one of the footman back home hadn't spoken in the same dialect, Susanna never would have made out the man's words. She glanced around for the owner of that accent. A man dressed as a dock worker swaggered up to her. He smelled as if his clothes hadn't been washed in a month.

"Looking for a little fun? A little coin?" he added in that same speech.

With barely a glance in his direction, she shook her head and stepped around him.

"I'm talking to you!" He grabbed her arm.

Alarm shot through her, lending her courage. "Release me at once."

"Ooooh, you talk all fancy like a real lady. Think you're too good for me, eh?"

She wrenched her arm out of his grasp and ran. In her haste, she nearly trampled a woman sitting on her doorstep.

"I'm so sorry," Susanna gasped. She glanced back but the man was sauntering the other direction.

The woman squinted at her and said in equally difficult to understand Cockney, "Poor lamb, ye don't belong 'ere, do ye? Come inside, pet, and I'll fetch ye a nice cup of tea." Though the words sounded kind, something in her tone and the gleam in her eye sent a chill through Susanna.

"No, thank you." She quickened her pace, heedless of the direction she took. She had been fortunate to have passed the night untouched, but her luck appeared to have run out. Perhaps her guardian angel considered her work complete. Where was that bakery?

A tea shop appeared nearby. Perhaps they had food, too. She headed for it. Black spots exploded before her vision. No, not again. She could not faint. Not here. Grabbing onto the side of a building, she tried to breathe through her dizziness.

A voice called her name from a great distance. The black spots grew and swallowed her whole and she floated into darkness.

Chapter Five

Kit barely managed to catch the little harpist before her head hit the ground. Completely limp and with a pallor somewhere between white and gray, she might have expired on the spot.

He patted her cheeks. "Miss Dyer? Susanna?"

No answer. Her colorless skin made her appear as if she had been made of paper.

Good heavens, this was no mere swoon. She appeared to be completely unconscious. A few passersby stopped walking and stared. This would never do.

"As you were," he snapped. He hailed a passing hackney. The jarvey eyed him as if he were some kind of villain who had just attacked the poor girl. "Take me to St. James place, at once."

He swung the nearly weightless unconscious form into his arms, scooped up the battered portmanteau she'd been carrying last night, and carried her to the hackney. Inside, he lay her on the seat and chafed her wrists, continuing to call her name. A full moment later, she roused, blinking.

She let out a cry of alarm. "Oh! Release me!" She struggled to sit.

"Don't be afraid, Miss Dyer, you are safe. Remember me? Kit Anson?"

She pressed a hand to her head and blinked at him. "Of course. I fear I..." She glanced about in confusion. "Where are we?"

"You fainted. Forgive me for my boldness, but I couldn't leave you to fall in the streets, and besides a crowd was forming. I thought an escape by hackney the best course of action. Where would you like me to take you?"

She pushed herself up and swung her legs off the edge of the seat. "I..." she took another breath. "You can take me someplace where I may purchase a bit of bread."

"Of course." He rapped on the door and stuck his head out to give a change of orders to the jarvey. That finished, he eyed her. Even so sober and frightened, she was still pretty. In fact, with such delicate features, a shapely mouth, and large gray eyes, she would be lovely if it weren't for her overly thin, alarmingly pale face and dark circles under her eyes. "Do you need a doctor?"

"No, not at all. I merely need to eat."

He nodded. "My mother sometimes swoons if she doesn't eat breakfast immediately upon arising, or if too much time passes between meals."

She fidgeted with her fingers. "Yes, that's it."

"I was about to have breakfast with my mother. Would you care to join us?" Of course, his mother might raise her brows at him bringing a ragged stranger, but it seemed rude not to invite her. And she was probably hungry.

She held up her hands in a warding position. "Oh, no, thank you. Really, you may let me off anywhere. I feel much better already."

He leaned back against seat cushions that had lost their padding years ago, and made a loose gesture out the window. "There is a nice little bakery on the next corner. He makes the best hot cross buns."

With a shaking hand she smoothed back her hair. "Thank you for the recommendation." She sat silently, tense and wary. Perhaps she feared for her reputation. Or his intentions.

"Do you have enough money for food?" He asked on a sudden whim. "If not, I could lend you—"

"Oh no, thank you. I have money for some bread."

Only for some bread? Was the poor girl literally starving?

"Mr. Anson—"

"Kit."

She faltered. "Kit. Do you happen to know where the Admiralty is located?" She fixed an earnest gaze upon him. She really did have the most remarkable eyes—gray with a little blue, and much brighter than one normally encountered, yet sad, almost haunted.

"Yes, I know where the Admiralty is. May I ask why?" It was bold of him to ask, but curiosity about the girl drove him to push the borders of propriety.

"I'm in search of news of my brother. He was a naval officer and he died at sea." She swallowed. "I was hoping to find someone to give me more information about him—whether he was buried at sea, and what exactly happened to him. I wrote to the Admiralty, but I never received an answer. I had hoped if I asked in person, someone might help me."

The carriage pulled to a stop in front of the bakery he had requested.

Strangely reluctant to part company with her, Kit stepped out and handed her down. "My brother-in-law works for the Admiralty. I could arrange for you to speak to him."

Her eyes lit up. "Would you do that?"

"Of course."

"I'm grateful to you. For everything." She smiled so brilliantly that he was momentarily speechless. By Jove, she really was a pretty little thing.

She picked up her portmanteau and stepped out of the carriage with all the manners of a fine lady, despite her dirty gloves and shabby clothes. Heedless of her appearance, she curtsied, thanked him again, and disappeared inside the bakery.

Kit paused, then cast a glance at the jarvey. "Wait here, please." He followed her inside and stood near the door behind her so she would not see him.

"How much for a loaf of bread?" Susanna asked.

Frowning, the baker gave her a once-over. "Two shillings."

"Oh." Her head lowered. "What can I buy with a farthing?"

"A plain brown bun." The baker held up a bun that Kit could eat in two or three bites.

"That will do." She handed over the money, accepted the paltry bite of food and turned away. She bit into it, closing her eyes and chewing as if she hadn't eaten in days. Perhaps she hadn't.

Kit stepped up to the counter beside her. Engrossed in her bread, Susanna made no indication that she saw him.

"Mornin', Kit," the baker said with a grin. "Come fer me hot cross buns?"

"Two, in fact. And I'll take two of your largest loaves of bread."

Susanna glanced up and met his gaze. Her face reddened, more color than he had seen in her. She swallowed and asked, "What are you doing here?"

"Buying bread. This is my favorite bakery, remember?"

Blushing again, she nodded and went outside. As

the baker got his bread and wrapped it in paper, Kit chatted with him, asking about his wife and sons, all the while glancing over his shoulder to keep track of Susanna outside the window. If she really were starving, he meant to do something about that.

Once outside, he gazed in both directions. Susanna had vanished. He looked down at the bread in his hand and sighed. He was too late to give it to her now, but he could give it to her tonight at the performance. Or better, yet, he would insist on taking her to the Silver Duck and see to it that she ate a full meal.

He gave a second set of instructions to the jarvey and sat lost in thought until the hackney deposited him at his parents' house, a stately home built in the style of country manner houses long before the city limits of London had reached out so far to encompass it. Once the carriage traversed the long drive amid two hundred-year-old trees and careful landscaping, the noises and smells of the city fell away.

Inside, the butler greeted Kit stoically and took his hat and coat. "Welcome home, Lord Christopher. Your mother is expecting you in the breakfast room."

Kit found his mother pouring tea. As he crossed the threshold, he stopped up short. She had aged. How was that possible? She hadn't had so many gray hairs when he saw her last year. A sense of her very real mortality seized him, along with the realization that his parents would not always be there. Pushing back such maudlin thoughts, he pasted on a smile.

"Mother, you look radiant as ever."

"Christopher!" She nearly knocked over her chair in her haste to reach him. He swiftly closed the gap between them and scooped her up for a hug.

"My darling boy," she said in a voice rough with tears.

His eyes stung at the affection in her tone. "Come now, it hasn't been all that long, has it?"

"A mother wants her children close by—even when they are grown. A year is far too long." She pulled back and took a good look at him. "You look well, son. So broad through the shoulders now. That is not a Westin coat, though, I'll warrant."

"Westin is a bit rich for my pocketbook now but I don't mind; there are precious few places I frequent where I would need to wear such a finely tailored suit."

"Oh, Christopher, come home and you can wear all the suits—"

"Now, Mother," he interrupted gently with a fond smile. "I'm not ready to relinquish my freedom just yet."

"As you wish." She laid a hand on his cheek and looked him over as if she had almost forgotten his features. "I'm so glad you've come. Do fill your plate and come sit."

As he picked up a plate at the end of the buffet table, he looked over the abundant selection with some amusement. "Are we expecting a dozen more for breakfast?"

"No, of course not. I just wanted to be sure all your favorites were present and that there was enough."

"Afraid I'm starving?" he quipped.

"Well, no ... but I'm grateful to see that you are not." She glanced at him. "You *do* have plenty to eat, do you not?"

He gestured to himself. "Do I look underfed to you?"

"No. Your color is good and you do look fit and well."

He loaded his plate, including a healthy selection of strawberries, as she filled him in on news about his brother, the estate, friends, and a few social issues. She waited until after he had eaten to broach what was clearly on her mind.

"My dear, I know you wanted to get out from under your father's thumb, but don't you think it's time to come home? I miss you."

He kissed her hand. "Mother, I miss you, and I promise to see you as much as possible while you are in London. But I am not coming home to subject myself to that intolerable tyrant."

"Your father only means to guide you to make the wisest possible decisions."

"I couldn't sneeze without his leave."

She sighed. "It's been two years. Perhaps there has been enough distance that he will allow you more liberties than before."

"Twenty years may not be enough distance."

A sad smile lined her mouth. "He means well, dear. He regrets his misspent youth and only wishes better for you."

"I know. And I assure you, I did not misspend my youth, nor am I doing so now. I am quite content making my own way in the world, independent of his control. I have steady work, and have made friends who seem to like me for who I am rather than my family tree."

She winced a little at his use of the word 'work' but only smiled gently as he finished. "You can't stay away forever, my dear. You need to remain involved in matters of the estate."

"Only Dunlap needs to involve himself in matters of the estate—that's an heir's purpose, don't you know? I am only the spare, which means I'm spared from such responsibilities." He smiled at his own pun.

A shadow passed over her face but she rallied. "You have never been merely the spare to me, son. I love both of my sons equally."

He squeezed her hand. "I know, Mother."

"Have you met a young lady yet, Christopher?"

The memory of the harpist with the clothes of a beggar and the smile and talent of an angel flashed through his mind. She was the only girl to have captured his interest in a very long time. "I don't socialize in the right circles for any of those entanglements. As far as my associates know, I am merely Kit Anson, a violinist. I spend my days with the working class."

She sighed delicately. "No, I suppose a suitable lady would not be amid that group."

If she only knew that the closest he had come to a lady in years was Susanna—a lady in every regard except, obviously, financial means, nor did he know anything about her family. For all he knew, her father might be a physician or a banker or even a factory owner.

"You *do* have comfortable accommodations and plenty to eat?" she pressed.

That was the third time she had asked if he had enough to eat. He grinned. "I have comfortable bachelor's rooms with a roof that doesn't leak, plenty of coal and candles, all the food I could eat, and sincere friends who don't toady up to me or try to outdo me—except, occasionally, my stand partner who wishes he were concertmaster. I couldn't ask for anything more."

"Except a relationship with your father."

True, but he refused to discuss that. "It's better this way. Tell me about yourself. Are you well?"

"Oh yes, except for the usual aches and pains and the annoying need to wear spectacles to read now."

Voices from the great hall attracted Kit's attention. His father. Time to leave. Kit kissed his mother's cheek. "Thank you for breakfast."

"I love you, Christopher."

He paused and took her hand. "I love you, Mother." He released her and departed through a side door.

Sooner or later he would have to speak to his father, but he planned to delay the inevitable as long as possible.

Chapter Six

Susanna awoke to voices and footsteps. Yawning, she stretched luxuriously. How lovely to finally sleep undisturbed, if only for a few hours. The floor of the opera pit had been a more comfortable bed than any she'd had in the previous ten days, ever since she left home.

"He's sweet on you, isn't he?" a feminine voice asked.

"Oh, aye," replied a second.

"And by your blush, you like him, too?"

"Aye, but I won't tell him. I must play coy lest he think I'm too easily won." A faint Irish accent gave her voice a musical lilt.

Susanna hurried to move out of the corner where she had napped away the afternoon, exhausted after spending hours looking for a room to rent. But with no money and no permanent position, she'd been refused at every turn. What would she do tonight?

They both giggled like school girls as they walked down the stairs to the orchestra pit. The only other female members of the orchestra walked past without noticing her. Susanna sat on the harp bench and ran her fingers up the strings in a soft glissando to check the strings' tune.

"Oh, my goodness, you scared me!" one of the young women exclaimed, looking at Susanna. "I thought we were the first ones here this eve."

Susanna smiled apologetically. "Forgive me for startling you. I arrived early. It takes a long time to tune."

She flushed. She hadn't exactly lied, just implied something other than the truth. She couldn't very well confess she'd slept in the orchestra pit because she had no place to stay at night. Still, she felt deceptive.

"Aye," said the other young woman. "I imagine with that many strings, it does."

"I didn't get a chance to introduce myself last night," the first one said. She smiled, revealing the whitest teeth Susanna had ever seen. "I'm Jane. I play viola. And this is Nora, a cellist."

Nora grinned and indicated the large instrument she carried on her back. "As if you couldn't guess."

Susanna smiled. "I thought it was either that or you were carrying a body." As the others chuckled, she added, "I'm Susanna, the temporary harpist."

Nora looked behind her and cocked her head. "Sleeping here, were ya?"

Susanna flushed and glanced back at the makeshift bed she had created out of her portmanteau, coat, and shawl. "I, er, took a nap. I wanted to be fresh before performance."

"Not sleeping well at night?" Jane took a step closer.

Susanna let out a little nervous laugh. "Not really, no."

Nora nodded sympathetically. "Are you new to London, then?"

"Yes, I arrived from the country only two days ago. I suppose I'm pretty green." Susanna ran her fingers along the harp's curved neck, similar to her harp back home but with different carvings, and made with dark wood.

Did she dare confide in these young women? If so, perhaps they could recommend a boarding house who might take her. Still, they were strangers. And Martha's warnings of the jealous and competitive nature of professional musicians were fresh in her mind. Nora and Jane seemed friendly enough, not the type to poison a competitor, but Susanna vowed to be careful, regardless.

Nora slid her cello off her shoulders and opened the case. "I never sleep well in a new place, either. Everything sounds and smells and feels different, it does."

"You brought your bag with you?" pressed Jane, glancing at Susanna's portmanteau.

Susanna flushed. "Yes, I always bring it." She could think of no reasonable explanation so she gave none. "It was a pleasure to meet you both." She picked up her tuner.

"You, too," Jane said. "I suppose as the only female members of the orchestra, we girls must stick together."

Susanna smiled, searching for the courage to ask if they knew of a place to stay. Other musicians filed in, talking and laughing. Jane and Nora chatted as they unpacked their instruments and warmed up. Susanna bit her lip. She had missed her chance. Perhaps after the performance.

Covertly, she slid the items making up her makeshift bed under the harp bench before she began the lengthy process of tuning.

"Are you feeling better, Miss Susanna?"

She glanced up at a pair of warm brown eyes and her heart did several flips. Truly her angels must have guided her to such a kind and handsome gentleman. "Mr. Anson."

He smiled. "Kit, please."

She got so lost in his handsome face that she almost forgot to answer his question. "I am feeling better, thank you. And thank you again for your assistance today."

"My pleasure." He shifted his grip on his violin case. "You mentioned you were new in town. If I can be of any assistance getting you settled, you have only to ask."

If he knew she had run away from home with little to her name and had slept last night in the streets next to a heap of refuse, he probably would not be so generous with his time. She dare not ask a man for recommendations for a woman's boarding house. That simply wasn't done.

"Thank you, er, Kit."

He studied her a moment longer, offered a brief bow, and moved up front to speak with the conductor, Alex. Susanna allowed herself the luxury of admiring Kit, his striking face, his lean, almost graceful form, his confident stance but without the swagger of an arrogant womanizer, like Percy. Kit certainly had been kind to her, more so than other men of her limited acquaintance.

Who was he? He spoke like a high born gentleman, and clearly had the benefit of an education. Of course, she daren't ask such personal questions.

"He's certainly a feast for the eyes, isn't he?" Jane smiled at her.

Susanna didn't know whether to be ashamed she had been caught mooning over him or relieved Jane shared her opinion. She settled for a guilty smile and a nod.

Jane continued, "I declare the first time I played with the orchestra, I was so distracted by looking at him that I could hardly pay attention to the music. Too bad I'm not right next to him where I can see him better. Then again, maybe it's just as well. I am married. Still, I have a good view from here." She let out a lusty sigh.

Susanna almost allowed herself a giggle before she stopped herself. Kit glanced back just then. Her face flamed at having been caught and she pretended to be absorbed in tuning.

He picked his way back to her. She considered whether she could truly sink into the floor but didn't know how to go about it.

When Kit reached her side, he said, "Alex said to tell you that the principal harpist is not expected to be healed enough to return for another few days, so if your performance is as good tonight, you have the job—temporarily."

"I do? Oh!" She clasped her hands together so she wouldn't embarrass herself by throwing her arms around him and hugging him. As it was, she barely managed to refrain from hopping up and down. "I'm ever so glad to hear it. I hope I will prove myself to Alex's satisfaction, then. And yours."

"You have nothing to fear."

"Thank you," she gushed. "Thank you again."

He nodded and returned to his seat. How wonderful! She had a position for the present time.

The performance went even better that night than the first, and Susanna immersed herself in the music. When the score called for rests for the harp, she watched Alex's animated gestures as he conducted. Once or twice—oh, very well, much more than that—she let her gaze stray to Kit. He swayed slightly as he played, and much of the time he closed his eyes as he poured his soul into his craft. Near the end of the first act, he played a solo. Susanna had never heard such beauty as Kit playing his violin. Such power and passion. The candlelit chandelier hanging from the domed ceiling shone on his dark hair, and the far chandelier backlit him, giving the illusion that he was some kind of heavenly being. Her father used to say angels played harps in heaven, and even called her 'his little angel.' Susanna was pretty sure they also played violins.

Pity no one in the audience could have the pleasure of watching Kit perform. The male singers on stage couldn't hold a candle to his masculine beauty.

When the score called for the harp, she joined in, blending her notes with the orchestra, and at the right moments, playing her glissandi. Then it was time for the harp and violin duet. She let her heart guide her, soaring with him as he soared, slowing and softening with him as if they performed an intricate dance with music instead of feet. A heavy weight lifted from her heart and dissipated like so much mist, carried away by the hauntingly beautiful pleasure of playing with Kit. A glorious sensation of being connected to him filled her, giving further emotion to her music.

By the time the last note faded away, a hush had fallen over the audience before thunderous applause nearly shook the theatre. He glanced back at her. She smiled and wiped tears from her cheeks.

With admiration shining in his eyes, he inclined his head in an abbreviated bow. If only she could always be so connected.

Alex broke the spell, cueing the prima donna who sang from stage and bringing in the orchestra. Still, a version of that wondrous sense of belonging lingered in Susanna's heart until after the performance.

As the final curtain fell and the orchestra packed up to leave, Susanna deliberated. Could she dawdle and then slip into the shadows so she could sleep in the orchestra pit, or did she dare ask Nora and Jane for their advice? She couldn't bring herself to face another night sleeping in an alley. The danger alone declared that a foolhardy plan.

Kit approached her, grinning. "I hope you will forgive me for saying so, but I'm glad the principal harpist was unable to perform. I never would have had the pleasure of playing with you. Don't get me wrong—

he is a very skilled musician, but you play with more feeling than I've ever heard from a harpist. That duet we played..." he trailed off and shook his head.

She shrugged, warming all over that he'd felt that same connection she had. "I merely followed your lead."

He smiled and a soft light entered his eyes. "Please allow me to buy you dinner at my favorite tavern. I'd really like to become better acquainted with you."

He wanted to become better acquainted with her? He couldn't mean that the way she thought. If only he did....

She held up both hands in an attempt to ward off temptation. "Oh, no. I couldn't impose."

"It would only be imposing if you refuse." He smiled disarmingly, a friendly, slightly teasing glint brightening his eye.

Still, she hesitated. How well, really, did she know him? Sure, he had helped her acquire the position as temporary opera harpist, he had come to her aid when she'd fainted, and he played the violin beautifully, but dare she trust him enough to go somewhere with him? Alone? All her life, she'd been cautioned to have a chaperone with her on the rare occasion she left home or if she ever were to entertain a male visitor.

Of course, she was no longer the cloistered daughter of a gentleman whose every move fell under public scrutiny.

Kit's demeanor changed, light in his eyes softened and turned almost pleading. Very gently, he said, "I realize you don't know me at all, but I give you my word as a gentleman that I will not allow any harm to come to you."

Her stomach chose that moment to growl.

He grinned. "You can't expect me to believe you aren't hungry."

Heat raced to her cheeks and she laughed softly. "I won't bother."

His grin widened. "I don't recall ever meeting anyone who blushed so easily."

She held her portmanteau in front of her with both hands. "It's my complexion. My mother used to say that people as fair as she and I are, are blessed with the gift of honesty—we can't tell a lie or even hide our feelings without turning red."

"She is as fair-skinned as you are?"

"Yes, she was." She let out a little sigh. "She was a great beauty." Rousing herself lest she fall into doldrums, she found a smile from somewhere inside her. "At least you won't have to worry if I'm being truthful with you."

"I wasn't worried. A late super then? With me?"

81

She glanced around. Nora and Jane were gone. So much for her plan to ask for their help. Her weakness and hunger warred with her hope to sleep safely inside the theatre. At the moment, her hunger won. She'd probably regret her choice later. Perhaps she could somehow get back inside tonight.

"Very well, I accept." She slid the cover over the harp and picked up her portmanteau.

He lifted a brow. "Do you carry that thing everywhere you go?"

"Of course." She lifted her head as if his had been a silly question, as if everyone carried baggage everywhere they went. He probably thought her odd.

"Then please allow me to carry it for you." He reached for her portmanteau.

She hesitated again. Everything she owned was in that bag, but if she could trust him enough to go somewhere with him, surely she could trust him with her bag and its meager contents. She surrendered her portmanteau.

With her bag in one hand, and his violin in the other, Kit wound through the orchestra pit to the stairs. Susanna followed him. As they reached backstage, he slowed his pace until she caught up with him. Then he matched his longer strides to her smaller steps. Jane and Nora stood in the wings, flirting with a pair of stage hands. They glanced at her as she walked past them next to Kit. Jane's mouth dropped open before curving into a delighted smile, and Nora's sentence trailed off.

Susanna walked a little taller next to Kit. It was silly, of course. He clearly had no real interest in her. No matter. Just being seen with such an admired—and admirable—man sent a flutter of wild tingles all over her. This would be one of the sweetest of Sweet Moments she could take out later to savour when she needed to buoy her spirits.

Chapter Seven

Unwholesomely pleased with herself at that moment, Susanna put her hand on Kit's arm as they worked their way to the exit. She had sacrificed another opportunity to ask Jane and Nora about lodging, but on Kit's arm, she couldn't muster up any regret. Besides, she would eat a full meal soon. Her mouth watered.

Kit called out a farewell to Bert at the door, and tucked the violin under the same arm that carried Susanna's portmanteau. As if it were second-nature, Kit opened the door and stepped back. He glanced expectantly at Susanna. She almost missed her cue. When was the last time a man had held a door for her? Her father, probably, had been the last, just as he always did for her mother.

To Kit, she murmured a breathless, "Thank you."

When they stepped outside into the cool London fog, Kit again offered her his free arm. Speechless at his thoughtfulness, she slipped a hand around his elbow and looked up at him. He stood a full head taller than she, and at that moment, appeared more knight than angel.

"Are you blushing again?" his amused voice rumbled softly.

She looked down. "This isn't a ballroom. You don't have to treat me like a fine lady, offering your arm and opening doors."

"Of course I do. The streets of London are almost as dangerous as ballrooms, you know." He grinned.

"I wouldn't know. I've never been to a ball."

"Outdoor country dances, then?"

"No, never." He must think her a backwards bumpkin.

"Really?" His brows lifted and a delighted smile brightened his already stunning face. "We must remedy that."

"Oh no, I haven't danced in so long, I doubt I remember how."

Her dance master had only worked with her for a few months before her parents both succumbed to influenza. Aunt Uriana, viewed Susanna's dance master an unnecessary expense and dismissed him. Later, Aunt hired a dance master for her daughter but forbade Susanna to participate.

Kit's voice drew her gaze. "Dancing is one of those delights in which everyone should have an opportunity to indulge. One can always learn—or relearn—the steps. Here we are." He led her to a tavern named the Silver Duck and held the door open. The Silver Duck. This was the same place with the pump in back where she'd been getting her water.

Inside, Susanna paused, breathing in the aroma of bread and beef stew. A few men clustered around tables drinking and talking. Some laughed raucously and others murmured, their heads close together. Tallow candles sputtered on the tables and in sconces on the walls but failed to provide more than tiny circles of light amid the darkness.

They found an unoccupied table and, always the gentleman, Kit held her chair out for her. After scooting her in and placing her portmanteau and his violin on an empty chair between him and the wall, he sat and turned a curious gaze upon her.

"May I ask you an impertinent question?"

She folded her hands in her lap. "You can ask, but I do not promise I will answer it."

"Fair enough. How does a gently-bred lady from the country end up in London playing for an orchestra?"

She opened her mouth, then closed it. How much to reveal? She tilted her head. "How does a gentleman with enough town polish who, if he wore the right clothes, could impress even the dragons who run Almack's, end up playing for an orchestra?" Of course, having never left her town until now, she knew little about such things except what she read in the gossip columns of her uncle's cast off newspapers.

He laughed uneasily. "*Touché.* Very well, I'll tell

you; I had a falling out with my father over a moral dilemma, and I left hearth and home to make my own way in the world—to prove to myself and to him that I am my own man and need not live under his tyranny."

Who was his father? A country squire? A distant relation to a lord? The more time she spent in his company, the less likely it seemed that he could be the son of a merchant or factory owner. From what she'd seen of society in her hometown and her aunt's guests, Kit had the kind of inherited polish of ancient gentry that families of new money never managed to capture.

Continuing his story, he said, "I needed a way of supporting myself so I auditioned for the opera orchestra."

"I see our stories and reasons are similar," she said.

Interest sparked in his eyes. "Have you been on your own long, then?"

"Not long."

His brow lifted as if he'd expected a different answer but he nodded. He laced his fingers in front of himself on the table top, his eyes searching hers. "Are you in some kind of trouble?"

"No. I merely...had to get away from my aunt's tyranny." Hopefully using his own words would stop the questions.

"It's one thing for a man to be on his own. It's another matter entirely for a lady to do so."

"A great number of women are alone."

"Not daughters of gentlemen."

She blinked.

He offered an apologetic smile. "Your manners and the quality of your speech give you away. When ladies fall on hard times, they usually find work as a lady's companion or governess so they are still under someone's care."

She weighed the wisdom of confiding in him. He seemed so kind, but he might think her wicked for refusing to marry the man of her guardian's choice and running away from home. The idea of losing his good opinion of her tied her tongue.

Finally, she managed, "I have had quite enough of being under someone's care."

"Ah, Kit." A rotund, rosy-cheeked man wearing an apron and wiping his hands on a towel emerged. "I wondered when you were going to show up. You brought a friend." His gaze flitted to Susanna. He looked her over curiously as if he couldn't imagine why such a plain little ragamuffin would be in Kit's company.

Addressing Susanna, Kit gestured to the man. "This is Ol' Joe. He and his wife own the place."

Ol' Joe's wife must have been the woman who

allowed her to wash using their water pump behind the building.

"Ol' Joe, this is Susanna. She's new to the orchestra. Plays the harp."

Ol' Joe lifted his brows. "Harp, eh? Never seen one of those up close. Bet it sounds like a little slice of heaven."

She smiled. "My father always thought so." A Sweet Memory returned, one of Papa sitting nearby, smiling, eyes closed, as he listened to her play, and Mama next to him, working on her sewing, also smiling. Fortunately for her, Uncle enjoyed it as well or her harp playing days would have ended years ago. Bless him, it was the one time he'd spoken up against his wife. He even had kept her supplied with a steady supply of new music.

"Are you hungry, too, miss?" Ol' Joe asked. "You could use some food, by the looks of you."

Heat crawled up her neck to her cheeks, and she lowered her gaze, nodding. Someday soon she'd find steady work and would eat on a more regular basis—enough to fill out like a woman instead of a scrawny little boy.

"We're both famished, Ol' Joe," Kit said.

The tavern owner nodded and disappeared behind a swinging door in back.

"You are a regular here, I presume?" she asked.

"This is one of the few places that serve food so late. I like their simple, wholesome fare."

Ol' Joe returned and placed the food on the table in front of them. Big chunks of beef, potatoes, and vegetables swam in thick broth. Susanna's mouth watered. She devoured the stew and a thick slice of brown bread Kit handed her. Oddly enough, she filled up faster than she'd expected considering how long it had been since she'd had a full meal. Perhaps her stomach had shrunk.

Pushing back her bowl, she let out a contented sigh and added the delicious meal with Kit to her Sweet Memories. Someday, she'd eat meals this satisfying every day with no one to lock her in her bedchamber without food.

Kit grinned. "I share the sentiment. I'm always starved after a performance." He stretched out his legs and folded his hands over his lean waist, still eyeing her. "I'm of a mind to take you to the public dance tonight, if you are willing. Will you come with me?"

"So late?"

"Many people go home early, but a fair number stay out late Saturday nights—probably because so many shops are closed Sundays; they can sleep in tomorrow. The music is good and the company is fun, if you don't mind associating with a working class rougher even than musicians." He offered a self-deprecating smile to let her know he wasn't truly a snob.

Who was Kit Anson? He had to have come from a family of means. His clothes were good quality, without holes or thinning places—not quite as fine as the members of the *beau monde* wore, but certainly among the prosperous working class. His manners and accent would fit in with even the upper crust of society. Clearly he'd been trained by the best; raw talent was one thing, but a musician of Kit's calibre developed from a combination of innate talent combined with years of training by the finest masters. Only someone with deep pockets would have the funds for a violin master to fine-tune his talent and mould him into a performer of unsurpassed skill.

He smiled. "You're thinking very hard about this. It's not supposed to be a difficult question."

She shook off her musings. "Of course I don't mind associating with the working class. I'm part of them. But I really don't remember how to dance. My dance master was dismissed years ago." She hadn't danced with a partner in so long—not counting her imaginary partner who danced with her each time she was confined to her bedchamber—she doubted she could do it properly. She'd probably embarrass herself.

"That's easily remedied. One can learn the steps

in a short lesson," he assured her. "A dance master probably wouldn't have taught you any of these dances anyway."

She cursed her wagging tongue. Now he knew she'd come from a family who could afford a dance master. She wasn't very good at remaining anonymous.

He leaned forward. "Do come. It will be fun. When was the last time you had a little fun?"

When, indeed? She took pleasure from playing the harp. She enjoyed walking along the river that ran through the estate—or at least, she did when she lived there. She liked reading. But fun? When was the last time she'd had fun?

Kit chuckled. "If it's taking you that long to remember, then you are overdue. Come." He stood, gathered up her bag and his violin, and held out a hand. "Dance with me." It wasn't a command, but rather an invitation.

Guided by the same reckless courage that had prompted her to leave her aunt and uncle, she placed her hand in his. "Very well. I will."

He gave her that infectious grin, and she couldn't help but smile in return. As if they were a fine lord and lady, Kit escorted her along the dark streets and alleys of London. With Kit at her side, the shadows no longer looked ominous, and passers-by seemed innocent of evil designs. Safe. This was what it felt to be safe in the presence of another person. How lovely.

A break in the buildings caught her eye and the gurgle of water beckoned to her. She stopped, straining to see what had caused it.

"Is that the river?" she asked.

"Yes, that's the Thames. Ever seen it?"

"Only at a distance."

"You'll want to see it, then. I can take you sometime during the day, if you'd like. The best place to view it is Wapping, down the old Waterman's stairs. I go see it every few days. It seems to pull me there." He smiled wistfully. "It's like an old friend to whom I must pay my respects. I never quite know what I'll find. Depending on the tide, it may be low and have an expansive beach, or so high and turbulent that one doesn't dare step off the stairs."

She admired his profile and smiled at his description of the river. "I would like to see that."

"Once when I was hungry, I found half a crown—the Thames' gift to me."

Susanna digested that. Such a refined gentleman, well-bred and well-educated, Kit had still shared some of Susanna's difficulties. The knowledge forged yet another connection with him. It somehow helped her feel less alone.

Following music, the buzz of conversation, and

the glimmer of lanterns, they arrived at a park. Kit led her to a wide open area filled with people dancing. Dancers twirled and laughed to the tune produced by the flute, horn, and lute. Based on the rough and even patched clothing, and even snatches of conversation she caught, the revellers appeared to be members of the working classes, all dancing and laughing with abandon, the likes of which Susanna had never seen when she'd snuck downstairs and peeked in on her aunt's soirees.

Kit walked up to the musicians. "Evening, Bob."

The lute player grinned, revealing several gaps in his teeth. "'Bout time, Kit. You gonna play wi' us?"

"Maybe later. For now, keep an eye on this, will you?"

He placed the portmanteau and his violin case at the foot of the lute player.

"Sure, sure. But you gotta at least play the last dance, something nice and slow."

"Of course." He held out his hand to Susanna.

He never grabbed her by the hand or arm; always offering his hand and giving her a choice whether or not to take it. She placed her hand in his and feared she was very much in danger of placing her heart in his hands as well. The warmth of the contact and the shivery little thrills that raced over her left her so winded she could hardly stand. Her whole being focused on his handsome face, the light in his eyes, the animated way he spoke, his scent of bergamot and mint, the resonance of his baritone voice. As he explained and demonstrated the dance steps, she had to remind herself to pay attention to his words.

He chuckled at whatever foolish expression she must have worn. "Let's just try it. You'll catch on as we go."

They wormed into the dance. Other dancers made room for them without batting their eyes. The current dance resembled a simplified country dance, and Kit was right; she did indeed learn the steps easily.

"I knew you could do it," Kit said.

He swung the woman to his left around as a man to Susanna's right swung her around. As her fears about the dance steps faded, since several revellers didn't appear to know the steps either, a new exhilaration filled her. Over the course of the night, she danced and danced and laughed and laughed, heedless of the gathering fog and almost total darkness except for a few lanterns. No one seemed to notice that all her dances began with Kit. How unlike the ballrooms of the *beau monde* where a lady daren't dance more than two sets with any given gentleman lest she risk being labelled "fast."

About the time her feet started to ache, the lute player began sending pleading glances to Kit.

He grinned and lifted a brow as he looked at Susanna. "Would you mind terribly if I played the last one?"

"Of course not," she gasped breathlessly.

"You don't have to sit out. I'm sure you could find a partner..."

"No, that's not necessary. I am in need of a rest."

She sat on the grass at Kit's feet. He picked up his violin, tightened his bow, and then drew it across the strings. A sweet, clear note rang out. The dancers quieted. He played a soft, slow melody, hauntingly beautiful, and the dancers responded in kind, seeking out sweethearts and holding each other close. He played. Sweet Memories of home and family surfaced in her mind—picnics in the sunshine with her family, riding or swimming with Richard, dancing on top of Papa's shoes when she was no taller than his waist, cuddles and stories with Mama by the fire or in her window seat.

A soft breeze cooled tears coursing down her cheeks. How fortunate she was to have such Sweet Memories when she no longer had her family!

As the final notes from Kit's violin faded away, she admired him anew. He was so kind, so gentle, so unrestrained in his joy as he lived the simple moments, and so willing to put his heart into his music instead of donning a cool, reserved exterior as so many English gentlemen were wont to do. A gentleman who chose to make his own way and spend his time with the working classes—befriending them even—was a rare man, indeed.

The more time she spent in his company, the more certain she was that he belonged somewhere amid gentry. His father must be a gentleman landowner. Did that place her in his class? Surely if he worked as a musician, he couldn't be so high on the social ladder. She did have a humble dowry—Aunt Uriana had said so.

No, best not think of it too much. Her dowry would not be enough to be a temptation to anyone—especially not to someone as elegant as Kit. She had little to offer. It didn't matter who her parents were when they lived. She was an orphan, a pauper with nowhere to sleep at night. She probably was as backwards and clumsy and stupid as her aunt had always told her. More tears streamed down her face.

As Kit lowered his violin, he looked into her eyes. He crouched down next to her and wiped her tears with the back of a finger. "Was my playing really that bad? Perhaps I should stick to dancing instead."

She laughed softly. "Not sad, exactly, just remembering my happy childhood long past." She looked down. With any luck, the darkness would hide her blush. After all, she couldn't exactly confess she wished she might qualify for a place in Kit's future. "Your music brought out some nostalgia."

He gave her a searching glance before he opened his case. Without speaking, he used a cloth to polish his violin, then, almost lovingly, laid his instrument inside, loosened the strings on his bow and put it away as well.

Emboldened by their closeness, she moistened her lips. "Tonight, you gave me many new Sweet Memories."

"Did I?" he sounded amused and pleased.

"A filling meal, dancing—what a delight that was—and your song. I will add them to my Sweet Memories that I always keep on hand so I can pull them out and relive anytime I wish to lift my spirits."

He touched her face. Some kind of tension she'd never known started in the pit of her stomach and her heart seemed alternately light and heavy.

"Good night to ye, Kit," the musicians called.

That odd connection broke and her face flashed hot. She looked down.

"Good night," Kit called. He picked up her portmanteau and held out an arm. They walked together, their steps muffled in fog swirling at their feet. "I suppose we all need our Sweet Memories. Perhaps I should make a conscious effort to collect them as you do."

She wound her hand through his elbow. "You seem naturally happy. I don't think you need to lift your spirits often."

"Not often. But there are times..."

"Your father?" she prompted softly.

He let out his breath. "He never failed to put me in a foul mood."

"Was it always that way? Have you no Sweet Memories of him? Not even when you were a child?"

He paused, and she bit her lip. Perhaps she should not have pried. As she opened her mouth to apologize and to retract her questions, he said, "It was different then. He was less critical, less condemning. He taught me how to shoot and fence and ride. We used to go fishing together. The first time I caught a fish, he acted like I'd won some kind of distinguished award."

She recalled Richard's pride when he carried home his catch of fish while Papa winked and praised him.

Kit shook his head. "But I grew up, and he disapproved of everything—my clothes, my friends, my love of music—I'm sure he thought it a passing fancy done to please my mother. And I disapproved of the use of slaves on our plantations in New Guinea." His face hardened. "If I were the heir, I'd shut those down and free the slaves."

Soberly, she studied him. Plantations in New Guinea. She knew it. His father was a powerful landowner, at the very least. "Is that why you left? You didn't want to spend any money he'd earned by using slaves?"

He nodded. "He was such a tyrant—wanted to dictate my every move. And yes, there are other ways to invest—the railroad, the canals, even factories up north, although I'd be selective about those as well. But yes, after going with him and my brother to the plantations and seeing first-hand how horrible slavery is..." He glanced at her. "My apologies. You don't want to hear this."

"Of course I do. You are a man of integrity, and I admire that in you." She snapped her mouth closed. Surely that had been too forward.

"You are blushing—I can see it even in this poor lighting. Did you just tell me a lie?"

Heat burned her cheeks hotter. "No. I fear I've been far too honest."

"Please." He stopped walking and turned to her, placing a hand over hers. "Please always be perfectly honest—especially when you are paying me a compliment." A teasing tone entered his voice, but she was so embarrassed that she couldn't look at him.

He chuckled and led her around a corner, where they literally ran right into a man with a large hat hurrying the other way.

The other man let out an *ooof* at the same time Susanna gasped. "I'm so sorry, sir," she said. "Pray forgive me."

"My fault, miss," the man with the hat said. Then he did a double take. "Susanna Dyer?"

She sucked in her breath. How did this man know her?

"You are!" He grabbed her arm. "Yer comin' with me, Lass."

Fear made her voice shrill. "Let go of me!"

"Release her at once." Kit's voice, though quiet, cut through the night.

The assailant glanced at Kit dismissively. "Not your concern, mate. Her family wants her back, and I'm gonna take her to 'em—now. See? I have this here picture." He waved a miniature at Kit, but in the darkness, he couldn't see it clearly.

"I am not going anywhere with you." Susanna tried to wrench out of his grasp and kicked him in the shin.

He grunted but didn't release her. "Not so fast, Lassie." He jerked her hard and seized her with both hands.

Kit's arm moved in a blur. The man went down, grabbing his throat and coughing.

Kit commanded in a voice she'd never heard him use, "Now leave at once before I summon a constable."

The man wheezed as he climbed to his feet. "Have a reward for her...bring her home...."

A reward? For her? Why on earth would her aunt and uncle do that? She would have thought Aunt would be happy Susanna had gone. Regardless, Susanna would rather starve to death a free woman than return to her prison.

Chapter Eight

All the breath rushed out of Kit's lungs. A reward for Susanna?

Now was no time for a discussion, and he refused to hand her over without hearing the whole tale. With years of boxing fuelling him, Kit swung his fist. The lawman went down with a string of curses.

"Come." Kit took Susanna's hand, tightened his grip on his violin case and her portmanteau, and they ran.

Dodging abandoned boxes and carts, piles of refuse, and even a few drunks snoring on the streets, they ran and ran until Susanna's breathing grew labored. She clutched her side, gasping. Kit spotted a hackney stand and called out for a cab.

After the drowsy jarvey loaded them inside a carriage, Kit said the first thing that came into his mind. "King's Theatre."

As the carriage rolled down the street, Susanna bent over holding her side and breathing heavily. Kit's thoughts skittered in circles. Had he been taken in by Susanna's seemingly innocent face and hard-luck story? She'd seemed sincere. He'd spent enough times in ballrooms and dinner parties, however, to discover many ladies had acting skills fit for the stage. In the two years since he'd left home, the memories of all those empty society games remained as bright as yesterday.

Still bent over, she gasped, "Thank you. That was frightening." Finally, she straightened. "I don't know if we would have escaped him if you hadn't acted."

He drew a breath, cooling his head. With the rush of energy still racing through him, and his sudden doubts about her, he purposely kept his voice soft, not entirely sure he managed to keep it gentle. "Are you in some kind of legal trouble?"

She blinked, then furrowed her brow. "No."

He rubbed his knuckles where he'd struck the man. He should not have risked hurting his hand, but striking out had been instinctive when he saw her in danger. "Then why is there a reward for your return?"

She let out a long, slow exhale. "The truth is, my aunt wanted to force me to marry her nephew, Algernon, but he's horrible. She threatened to lock me in my bedchamber until the wedding. So I ran away." She shook her head. "I can't believe it's so important as all this, though."

Her words buzzed around his head like mindless insects. *Forced. Marry. Horrible. Locked away.*

She spread her hands. In the darkness, he could not decipher her expression. "And surely Percy doesn't want me to be his mistress badly enough to go to so much trouble, especially when there are so many courtesans he could surely...acquire."

Shooting a glance at him, she fidgeted with her hands the way she always did when she blushed. She probably blushed because of the mention of courtesans, but he couldn't quite dismiss the fear that she was lying. Had he been duped by a master of deception?

Kit gripped his violin case until his fingers ached as a thousand questions roared through his mind.

Susanna seemed to fold in upon herself. "No one wants to inherit a poor relation when they inherit a property. Now that her daughter is about to come out, my aunt doesn't want me underfoot." As they passed a streetlamp, the light illuminated her face and shone on her eyes filling with tears. She whispered, "I'm an embarrassment to her."

Kit softened at her words. He couldn't imagine her being an embarrassment to anyone. She was perfectly poised and gracious, even in a lowering situation. Her manners were impeccable. She spoke with the cultured accent and musical tones of a queen. Adding to that her talent of playing the harp like an angel, she had much to offer. She was even prettier than he'd first believed. One burning question remained; was she being honest with him?

He shook his head. "I still don't understand. If she only wanted you gone, why would she go to all the trouble to offer a reward for your return?"

She shook her head. "I cannot imagine. She was always going on about how she wished I were no longer her concern."

"And this...Algernon." Kit wished a pox on the man. "He is in love with you and wants you to come back?"

She let out a derisive huff. "No. Honestly, we've scarcely conversed. I usually find an excuse to keep out of his sight when he visited. He simply needs a wife to become a vicar as per the terms of that particular vicarage. I suppose my aunt begged him to take me off her hands as a way to help them both."

"So he wants to take you for his wife in order to be appointed as a vicar?"

"It seems so. There certainly is no affection between us, and my dowry is not much of a temptation. Although, I suppose for a vicar, it might be adequate." She shivered. "I cannot—will not—marry him, no matter what she does to me."

Memories of his father's bullying awakened new sympathies toward her. If she were honest, if her aunt really were trying to force a marriage, he couldn't blame Susanna for balking. Or running.

He tried to gentle his voice, but fear that she'd

been playing some game with him edged into his voice. "Why is he so undesirable?"

"Not only is he sixteen years my senior, he's rude and thick-witted and he has gout. More importantly, he is unkind in every regard." She grimaced. "He strikes servants, he slaps maids on their, er, in an inappropriate place, and I've seen him be cruel to animals."

Kit's opinion of the unknown man fell even further. A man such as he would surely make Susanna miserable...if she were all he thought she was until moments ago. "You can think of no other reason they want you back badly enough to send someone after you with the offer of a reward?"

She shook her head. "I suppose if the banns have already been read, they're trying to spare themselves some embarrassment. I can't imagine why else. My aunt made it clear she wanted me out of *her* house," she choked, "as soon as possible."

He felt a beast pushing her, but he had to be sure. "You didn't...take anything when you left?"

"Only a change of clothes, a miniature of my parents, a few pins, my brother's letters, and my mother's wedding ring." Her lower lip trembled. "I sold my pins and my mother's ring in a village outside of Bedford to buy my ticket for the mail coach. It was so lovely, gold and sapphire—the only thing I had of hers." Her voice faded. She sighed and shook her head. "I saw no other way."

Even in the semi-darkness, tears on her cheeks became visible. Silently, she wiped her cheeks. If those were tears of an actress, she was certainly playing it subtle. He wanted to believe her. She seemed so genuine. Dancing with her had been a rare delight. He'd become aware of her on a deeper level—cared for her on a deeper level—than he had experienced before.

Why would her relatives send someone determined to drag her back home? Something didn't fit. "And you took nothing else—nothing of value, even if you considered it yours for the taking?"

"No. The miniature of my parents in my portmanteau can't be of much value to anyone other than to me." She paused. Her breathing changed. "You think I'm a thief?" The shock and hurt in her voice could not be mistaken.

"Why are they so desperate to get you back if they value you so little?"

She glared at him. He offered a challenging, searching look of his own. Hurt, mixed with anger, revealed themselves in her expression.

She straightened and lifted her chin. Indignantly, she said, "You are right—I have no value to them. I don't know why they want me back. If you don't trust me and you truly believe me a criminal, then we have nothing to say." She banged on the door. "Stop the coach!"

Before he realized what she was about, she grabbed her portmanteau, opened the door, and leaped out before the coach had fully stopped. She hit the street with a thud and a tangle of skirts and rolled. Instantly, she got up and ran.

"Stop!" Kit yelled. He barely had the presence of mind to grab his violin case before he leaped out after her.

"Oi! Me fare!" the jarvey yelled.

"I'll be back—wait here," Kit called over his shoulder. He charged after her, following her thin, shadowy form as it dashed ahead into the fog. "Susanna, wait!"

No reply. No motion.

He slowed to a stop. Where had she gone? Between darkness and fog, he could barely see even familiar landmarks. "Susanna?"

No response. Still, she had to be nearby. A dog barked. A male form strode past.

Kit tried again. "Susanna, I'm sorry. I didn't mean to question your character, but I don't know you very well—it's only been two days. Well, two nights." Egad, that came out wrong. "Two evenings. And a short time this morning." Good grief, now he was babbling. "It's hardly long enough to really take measure of someone's character."

"Quiet down there!" someone hollered from an open window.

He lowered his voice. "Please come back. I won't leave you here alone."

He waited, his thumping heart the only detectable sound. Then, finally, a rustle. A tiny form stepped out of the shadows.

"I am not a thief." Her voice, calm and firm, spoke as sweet as music.

He released his breath, only just then realizing how frightened he'd been that she might have run so far that she was alone and unprotected in the streets.

"I took nothing that belongs to them." Her firm voice rang of truth.

"Forgive me. I had to hear those words from you to know for sure."

She made no move.

He held out an arm. "Come, it's not safe here. I'll take you home."

She folded her arms. "That's not necessary. I can find my own way." Her indignant tones might have made him smile if the situation weren't so grave.

"It's two o'clock in the morning, and we're in an unsavoury part of town. I am not leaving you here unprotected."

She said nothing.

He held his breath. If she refused, he just might

110

toss her over his shoulder and carry her to safety. She'd probably scream and alert the night watch, however, and that would create more trouble than he wanted.

He tried again. "I believe you, Susanna—I don't think you are thief. Please come with me."

She threw up her hands and grumbled, "Very well—only so you'll leave me in peace."

He remained motionless as she moved to his side, but she folded her arms rather than take his. Whether she did it to make a point or out of an attempt to stay warm in the chilly, damp night, he could not decide. He removed his coat and placed it over her shoulders. She stiffened. He half-expected her to throw off his coat. Instead, after a pause, she unfolded her arms and snuggled into it. He gestured to her portmanteau and held out a hand. Again a pause. Finally, she relinquished it to him. He switched it to his other hand so she could take his arm if she chose. She did not. Side-by-side, they walked silently back to the waiting hackney. He handed her in and took the rear-facing seat. She remained folded in on herself.

Inside the hackney, he set his violin case and her portmanteau on the seat next to him. "Where do you want me to take you?"

"You can take me to the King's Theatre. I can walk from there."

So she didn't want him to know where she lived. He supposed he couldn't blame her, but it stung. After he called out instructions to the jarvey, they rode in silence.

They arrived at the impressive structure on Haymarket and stopped in front of the arches. Kit glanced up at the tall columns gracing the second floor of the King's Theatre and then peered down the street. To his knowledge, there were no suitable living spaces nearby. She had to be staying somewhere in the area because she always seemed close at hand.

"Where, exactly, shall I leave you?"

"This is adequate." She snatched up her portmanteau, opened the door and stepped out before he had a chance to help her. She took several steps in the opposite direction from where she'd walked last night and then turned around. "You may go now."

"Why are you so concerned that I discover where you live? Surely you don't think I'm the kind of scoundrel who would force my way into your chamber."

She shifted her hold on the portmanteau. "No."

"Are you worried I'll reveal your whereabouts to your family or that man who made a grab for you?"

She stiffened. "Would you?"

"No." His outraged tone of voice raised more than he'd intended. Why must she be so vexing?

112

She softened her voice. "Thank you. And thank you for dinner. And for dancing. Good night."

She turned to leave. After a few steps, she stopped and returned to him. Looking steadily at him, Susanna removed his coat and held it out to him. She waited until he gave the jarvey the order to proceed before she started walking again.

He watched her through the back window as they drove away. She stood alone for a long moment, her small form shrinking. She finally started walking, but then took a sudden turn and dashed to an alley. Her furtive movements raised his suspicions.

He stuck his head out and addressed the jarvey. "Stop. Wait here."

The jarvey no doubt thought he was mad, but complied. Kit got out. Stepping softly, he followed in the direction he'd seen her take. There, her thin form still moved. Sticking to the shadows, he tailed her, fog billowing with each step. Next to a stack of wooden boxes, she stopped. Kit flattened himself against the wall and held his breath. She looked around, then slid down to the ground and tucked her feet under her. Hugging herself, she crouched, her breath ragged in the night. Nearby a cat crept out and slunk along the alley. Male voices, low and rough, murmured. Someone laughed. A baby cried and hushed. The truth of her situation slapped him in the face. He'd suspected she had gone hungry, but never imagined she had nowhere safe to sleep. The idea twisted in his gut. No one should be so desperate.

"This is why?" he said.

She shrieked and stood.

He stepped out of the shadows so she could see him.

She let out a combined gasp and sigh. "Kit?"

"How long have you been sleeping in the alleys?" he demanded.

With a sob, she put her hands over her face. "I'm so humiliated."

He approached and asked gently. "There is no reason for embarrassment. I'm merely...surprised."

Without removing her hand, she sighed, sad and resigned. "The theatre manager refused to give me an advance except for the farthing I used to buy my bread this morning. None of the respectable boarding houses I tried would take me without a letter of introduction or a week's payment in advance."

Aghast, he stared, still grappling with her reality. Then finally, he managed, "Why didn't you tell me?"

"I was too ashamed to tell anyone." She stood hugging her portmanteau, her shoulders slumped.

"You're lucky you didn't get robbed, or...worse."

"I don't have much choice. I'd hoped to remain behind and sleep in the theatre tonight but I couldn't pass up the opportunity for a meal."

114

He took a step closer. "Now that you're finally being honest with me, how long since you have eaten?"

"I have been honest with you. I just didn't volunteer certain information."

"How long, Susanna?"

She chewed her lower lip. "I had a plain bun this morning."

"And before that?"

She paused. "I had a bit of bread pudding two days ago."

His stomach clenched. "And before that?"

She huffed. "Why does that matter? As soon as I start earning money, I can eat a proper meal every day."

"It matters because you look as if you haven't eaten a proper meal in weeks—or longer."

She said nothing.

Kit paced. He couldn't leave her here like this. There were a few reputable boarding houses but they wouldn't take her in the middle of the night even if he offered them a great deal of money. His mother would probably take her in, but she'd misunderstand his intentions toward the girl. And his father would be an overbearing snob to her. His sister? Now that was a possibility. She and her husband would be gracious about giving Susanna a place to sleep until

115

Kit could find more permanent lodgings for her. Of course, if he took Susanna there, she'd eventually figure out who he was. However, no better solution presented itself.

He held out a hand. "My sister lives nearby. She would be happy to let you stay with her until other arrangements can be made." He smiled. "She'll probably invite you to stay for the whole Season."

Susanna shook her head. "I cannot impose."

"Trust me, she will love it. Esther will make you feel welcome. She loves to feel needed and is always going about throwing herself into one cause after another." As a child, she often brought home stray kittens and fallen birds and injured rabbits.

"I am not someone's cause. I'm tired of being a pawn to forward the interests of others."

He almost cursed out loud. "I didn't mean you were a cause. I only mean that she'd love to help you."

"I don't want her charity," she said flatly. "I'm sick to death of relying on someone's charity."

"Your aunt's so-called charity, for example?"

After a moment's silence, she said in a hushed voice, "She was always going on about how ungrateful I was and that only her charity kept her from throwing me out to find my own way."

The idea of such a dragon raising this sweet little thing made Kit grind his teeth. "My sister isn't like that. She'll love you." He wiggled the hand he held out to her. "Please come. If you don't, I'll be obliged to stay out here all night to watch over you. And what about that man determined to drag you back to your aunt?"

Her posture changed at that reminder. "We can't show up to your sister's house now—as you said, it's two o'clock in the morning."

"She should be arriving home from her ball or soiree right about now; she's not one to dance until dawn."

Silently, Susanna studied her feet and then looked up as if the night sky held answers she sought. Still holding his hand out, he took several steps closer to her. At his approach, she looked directly into his eyes. In the pale light of the moon slipping in and out of clouds, the sharp planes of her cheekbones as well as the hollows under her eyes softened. Her eyes appeared overly large and mysterious and somehow timeless, as if she were some mystical being who'd taken on the appearance of a young lady. This was no waif; she was a strong, determined woman who faced her challenges with courage and grace. He doubted many young ladies of the *ton* were in possession of her depth of character and resiliency.

He could fall in love with such a lady.

He wiggled his fingers. "You will like Esther.

117

She's very kind. If her own brother can say such a thing, it must be true, right?" He grinned.

A hint of a smile passed over her. Still, she made no move to take his hand. Instead, she continued staring warily at him.

He tried again. Gentler now, he said, "It would only be until you can find a place of your own."

Her posture wilted as the fight drained out of her. "Very well." She placed her hand in his.

As he wrapped his fingers around her small hand, a surge of protectiveness overcame him. Why he felt so compelled to help this near-stranger, he could not explain. Perhaps it was her desire to be independent that awakened a kinship in him, since he'd left his home with the same goal. A man trying to make it alone in the world was much less vulnerable than a young woman who attempted such a thing.

He almost smiled at the lie he tried to tell himself. He wanted to help her because he had grown to care about her—much more than he thought possible in such a short amount of time. She was fiercely independent and courageous, despite her desperate need, and made the best of her circumstances. He smiled as he recalled the way she'd shown up at the theatre, insisting she deserved a chance. Yet the vulnerability in her eyes tugged at his heart. Yes, he was, indeed, growing to care very much about Susanna Dyer.

They walked hand-in-hand like children down the middle of the streets, their steps falling in sync. Her small hand in his felt so very right, as if it had been designed for his and he'd only now discovered he'd been missing a part all this time.

Fog swirled at their feet, and a bell clanged off in the distance. Two young men staggered past them, arms linked and singing a bawdy song. Kit kept hold of her hand, tuned in to even the sound of her breathing.

"Is it far?" she asked.

"No. Just a few blocks over."

Quietly she asked, "Why are you helping me, Kit?"

He grappled for an answer that would not make him sound mad or raise her expectations until he could determine, what exactly, his intentions were toward her. "Because my mother raised me as a gentleman."

She smiled, clearly not quite believing his words. "Surely there is more to it than that."

"That is a pretty compelling reason. 'Tis my duty—my honor requires it."

"Oh." Her face fell. "Well, then I thank you, but your obligation to me does not need to continue. I do not wish to be so indebted."

"You are not indebted. People helped me after I

left home. I am returning the favor the only way I can."

A few minutes later, they arrived in front of his sister's house. Kit led her up the steps to the front door.

Susanna slowed her steps as she looked up at the elegant, tasteful structure. Her mouth dropped open. "Your sister lives here?"

He couldn't decide if she were awed or frightened. He sent her a quick smile. "Yes, but don't hold it against her."

As luck would have it, the moment he reached for the doorknocker, his sister's coach arrived. Turning, he watched his sister and brother-in-law emerge, laughing. They walked arm-in-arm toward the front door. As his sister caught sight of Kit, she released her hold on her husband's arm and trotted up the last few steps.

"Kit!" She threw her arms around him. "How wonderful to see you."

He chuckled. "I saw you last week, as I recall, Tess."

"I'm just as happy to see you now! Come in, come in."

"First, allow me to introduce Miss Susanna Dyer. She is the harpist for the time being in my orchestra and a gifted musician. Susanna, my sister, Esther

120

Daubrey." As his brother-in-law climbed the rest of the way up, watching them with an air of sophisticated amusement, Kit said, "And her husband, Robert Daubrey."

Daubrey lifted his brow slightly at Kit's omission of his title, but voiced no complaint.

Susanna curtsied prettily and said in low, musical tones, "A pleasure to meet you both." Her fine breeding practically oozed from her.

With only a thinly-concealed look of delight aimed at Kit, Esther leaped to action, beaming at the unsuspecting girl. "Susanna, how lovely to meet you. May I call you Susanna? You don't look like the type to stand on ceremony, but it if makes you uncomfortable, I can certainly call you Miss Dyer."

Blinking at the flow of enthusiasm, Susanna smiled. "Susanna suits me just fine."

"Then you must call me Esther. Or Tess. Do come in."

Daubrey gave Kit a sidelong glance but followed Esther inside. Kit almost groaned out loud. His sister was probably already making wedding plans. He should have known she'd be as bad as his mother. And worse, his secret would be out soon and everything with Susanna would change.

Chapter Nine

Susanna grappled at her composure and tried not to gape like a country bumpkin at the splendor around her. The foyer surpassed the great hall back home with its sweeping ceilings, carved and gilded woodwork, marble floor, and a circular staircase out of a fairy tale. Potted plants and flowers scattered amid the gleaming surfaces softened the almost blinding grandeur. Was this awe-inspiring structure the home of a member of the *ton*, or a purchase by someone who'd made a fortune in trade? Either way, this mansion exceeded her childhood home in both size and opulence.

A surprisingly young butler took their coats and her portmanteau as Esther Daubrey, a trim, dark-haired lady near Susanna's age, addressed the butler. "We'll take refreshment in the back parlor." She linked arms with Susanna and led her across the floor. "You simply must tell me about yourself." She turned sparkling eyes, the same rich brown color as Kit's, upon her.

With a nervous laugh, Susanna said, "There's not much to tell."

"Oh, don't be modest. How on earth did you

obtain a position as impressive as the harpist for an opera symphony? That's quite an accomplishment, you know, especially for a woman."

Susanna shrugged. "It's not a great story. I happened to present myself at an opportune time; their harpist injured his hand, and they were desperate for a replacement. Although, to tell the truth, your brother kindly convinced the conductor to allow me to audition. Without him, I would never have been allowed inside the theatre. He must have been the angel for whom I had been praying."

"My brother Kit?" Esther laughed. "That may be the first time anyone has called him an angel."

"You should have heard her play, Tess; she silenced Alex." Kit's baritone rumbled from behind them.

"You must be truly magnificent, then. I've heard much about this Alex." Esther led her to a floral settee near the fireplace. "It's chilly tonight, isn't it? So tell me; from where do you hail?"

"The nearest village is Bedford, in the Thames Valley."

"And you are here for...what purpose? The Season?" She cast only the briefest glances at Susanna's shamefully out-of-date and threadbare gown but her expression did not reveal her thoughts.

"I came to find a position as a harpist. I intend to make London my home."

123

Something almost calculating, but not in a cold way, entered Esther's eyes, as if she were fitting together pieces of a difficult puzzle. She was probably trying to figure out why her brother, who was obviously from money, spent time in the company of a penniless nobody garbed in clothes a scullery maid would have been embarrassed to wear in public.

Esther nodded. "How long have you been in London?"

"I arrived a few days ago."

"And already secured a position as the orchestra's harpist." Esther smiled as if Susanna had achieved some miraculous feat. Which, really, she had—but only with Kit's help.

Susanna clasped her hands together. "It's only until the orchestra harpist returns, but I hope to have secured something long-term by the time they no longer need me."

Esther nodded, watching her with mingled curiosity and amusement. Did she think Susanna was a completely green country girl? Or did her need of employment place her so far below Esther's circle of friends that she might have well been a footstool?

Kit took a seat in a nearby armchair. "I'm sure you will find something by then."

Esther glanced at him. "You know you are welcome any time, Kit, and I adore that you've brought me a new friend, but I suspect you aren't here at this hour to make a simple social call."

Kit's mouth quirked into a grin and he exchanged glances with Susanna. "Right, as usual."

Susanna's mouth dried. She couldn't possibly stay here amidst such opulence. She was now a member of the working class. She only owned two gowns, neither of which were fine enough for Esther's servants, much less people in her social circle. Perhaps Esther would let her work here in some capacity. The problem was, Susanna had few skills and no knowledge of how to work as a servant.

Susanna shot to her feet. "Kit wanted me to meet you, that's all. We really must be going. I am sure we are keeping you from your beds."

Kit stood and reached for her hand, giving her a quelling look while still speaking to his sister. "Susanna has not yet found a suitable place to live and I was hoping you could allow her to stay here until she makes more permanent arrangements."

Susanna rushed in, "But of course, this would be a terrible imposition on you and I—"

"Of course you can stay here," Esther said. She glanced at her husband standing near the fireplace.

Daubrey inclined his head in return, his eyes alight as if he watched a diverting theatrical presentation. "Certainly."

Susanna shook her head. "When Kit told me about you, I was expecting something less..." she gestured around at the parlor, its furnishings, the display of wealth. "Like this."

Esther waved her hand negligently. "Oh, don't mind this. Most of this old rubbish is a hundred years old and either in need of cleaning or updating. This big house and only the two of us, why it's a waste. We'd be so pleased to have you stay here as our guest for as long as we can keep you." She laid a hand on Susanna's arm and leaned forward. "Do say you'll stay. Not many of my friends are in town yet so I was dreading a lonely existence over the next few weeks until they arrive for the Season."

Susanna glanced at Kit's determined expression, and at Esther's beseeching face, and lastly at Daubrey.

With a fond look at his wife, he took a pinch of snuff and said, "You'd best agree with her, Miss Dyer, or she'll pester you until you give in anyway."

Susanna let out a long breath. What choice did she have? She could sleep in the streets, with Kit dogging her every step, or she could race out into the night. Or, as they urged, she could be gracious, at least for tonight. Perhaps she'd find accommodations on the morrow.

She smiled self-consciously at Esther. "Thank you so much for your hospitality. I promise I'll try not to be a bother."

Esther clasped her hands together. "Oh, I'm so pleased and I'm certain you will be a sheer delight. Now that you are here, I have someone to go with me on walks and shopping expeditions. It will be so fun! Have you ever been to London before?"

"This is my first time," Susanna said.

A tray of food arrived laden with oranges, strawberries, scones, Devonshire cream and jam along with tea. While Esther murmured instructions to the maid who nodded and slipped away, Susanna feasted on the delicious food. Her aunt seldom let her enjoy such a wonderful repast, citing that such fine foods were not to be wasted on poor relations. As Susanna ate the formerly forbidden foods, Esther outlined places she wanted to take Susanna.

They sounded truly marvelous, but how could she visit all those places in the company of a fine lady? Why, her gowns alone would be an embarrassment. And what if she really were stupid and backward as her aunt had told her for years?

Kit smiled at her over the tray. Susanna shot him a look of panic, but he only broadened his smile. He sat conversing with Daubrey, but his gaze returned to her with unsettling frequency. If she could manage to stop gawking at him for even a few minutes, she might not be so aware of his glance. In this room, in this world, he seemed as comfortable as he had been dining in a common tavern or as the concertmaster of a noted orchestra. His self-possession and assurance combined with his handsome face created an intimidating façade for such a kind and generous man. She had suspected early on that he was a member of one of the upper classes by birth, but entering his sister's house had confirmed it. Despite his present occupation, he was clearly so far above her level that she could hardly believe he took enough interest to feed her and find her lodgings. Why had he even stooped to speak to her, desperate and ragged as she was?

Because he was kind, that's why. No other reason.

Once they'd eaten their fill, Esther stood. "You must be as tired as we are. Come, I'll show you to your bedchamber. It should be prepared by now."

Susanna glanced at Kit. "Good night. And thank you."

He bowed over her hand like a gentleman bowing over the hand of a lady. "It is my pleasure. Sleep well." He handed the portmanteau to her.

She smiled when she wanted to weep. "I hope you do as well. Thank you for your kindness."

Kit kissed his sister's cheek. "Don't wear her out dragging her all over town, Tess. She has performances every night except Sunday."

"Of course, of course. Be off with you." Esther waved her hand.

After a final glance that sent a tingle clear down to Susanna's toes, Kit left.

Again, Esther linked arms with Susanna and led her upstairs. "I'm so glad you're here, Susanna. I hope you don't hurry overmuch to find another place to live."

In what was surely the family wing, Esther brought Susanna to a lovely room much like her old bedchamber years ago. Soft pinks and rose adorned the bed and pillows on the chairs amid the Georgian-style furnishings. A cheery fire crackled in the fireplace, and candles burned on every table top.

When was the last time she'd been allowed more than one candle in her bedchamber? Such luxury!

Esther nodded at a maid who poured water from a bucket into a china pitcher. "I apologize for how small it is, but the larger rooms would have needed more time to prepare."

"This is beautiful," Susanna said in an awed voice.

"Polly will assist you with anything you need."

Polly, a trim girl with dark hair, bobbed a curtsy, and folded her hands together to await instructions.

Esther hugged Susanna quickly. "I hope you are comfortable and happy here, Susanna."

Susanna set down her portmanteau. "I can't thank you enough for your generosity—especially on such short notice."

"I'm so glad you let Kit and me bully you into staying here." She grinned and swept out of the room.

Polly sprang to life. "There's hot water here if you wish to take a sponge bath, miss."

Susanna blinked. "I do, indeed." She could hardly wait to peel off her clothing after traveling and sleeping in the street. "But you needn't help me. I can do it."

"It's my pleasure, to serve you, miss."

Polly set up a screen in front of the fire. As Susanna started to remove her gown, Polly hurried over. "Allow me, miss."

Susanna faltered but allowed Polly to help her out of her gown, unlace her short stays, and remove them along with her chemise. What must the maid be thinking of Susanna—so dirty and ragged and showing up unexpectedly in the wee hours of the morning?

Susanna blushed at the attention and at being so unclad in the presence of another person. However, Polly's efficient, no-nonsense manner eased her discomfort by degrees.

Susanna scrubbed herself with a sponge until her skin turned red. The wash water turned an embarrassing color of dirt. Oh, how glorious to be clean! She smiled at the thought that something she'd once taken for granted could now be such a delicious indulgence.

Polly said, "Tomorrow, if you wish, I will have a hip bath brought in."

A bath. A full bath. She sighed. The luxury of immersing herself in warm water taunted her like a sweet dream. "Oh yes, please. My hair needs washing, too. But you needn't go to so much trouble. I can do it."

Polly held a towel to Susanna. "No trouble at all, miss."

"I wouldn't dream of you carrying up all those buckets of water. I can bathe in the kitchen, can't I?"

The maid paused. "If you don't mind my asking; haven't you ever had a lady's maid?"

"No. As a child, I had a nursemaid. When I was thirteen, my aunt and uncle became my guardians. They dismissed my nursemaid because they said poor relations should be more self-reliant."

The maid nodded sympathetically. "Well, as long as you are here, I am pleased to serve you, and that includes having a bath brought into you any time you desire. If it makes you feel better, I am not required to do the carrying—that's for the footmen to do."

Susanna nodded but still regretted having to ask some poor young men to carry all that weight up several flights of stairs.

"Or if you prefer," Polly added, "You can bathe in the shower-bath like Lady Daubrey does."

Susanna froze. "*Lady* Daubrey?"

"Yes, miss. My lord's father had the shower bath installed a year ago—quite a clever invention. My lady likes it ever so much."

Susanna barely noticed talk of the shower bath. Her attention focused on the title and the seed of suspicion that her hosts were more than she'd first believed now grew into a sapling. "Your lord is who?"

A brief flash of confusion slipped over the girl's features. "Lord Daubrey. Didn't you know?" She blushed and stammered, "Forgive me for my impertinence, miss."

Weakly, Susanna managed, "No, it's quite all right." Still, just to be sure, she asked, "Robert Daubrey is a titled lord?"

"That's right, miss." The poor girl glanced about as if she feared she were in the presence of a bedlamite.

"And Esther Daubrey is a titled lady?"

"Yes, miss."

Wrapped in a towel, Susanna sank into the nearest chair. A lord. A lady. Good heavens. The full impact of whose hospitality she'd accepted finally hit her. She should have known. She had imposed on nobility like some kind of lost puppy too desperate and naive to know better.

Weakly, she asked, "What exactly is Lord Daubrey's rank?"

"He's a viscount, miss."

Who, exactly, was Kit that his sister married a peer? Was she the daughter of a gentleman who'd married above her class? Or was Kit's family a member of the *beau monde* by birth? If so, that would explain much. It would also generate more questions. She really must find out more about him. Kit must have suspected if he told her such a crucial piece of information she would never have agreed to come.

She wanted to put a hand over her face. She had not only appeared on the doorstep of Kit's sister, but that of a titled lord and lady. She moaned out loud. Based on her appearance and state of need, they must think her some kind of gutter rat trying to ingratiate herself into the world of her betters.

Still, Esther had been an unexpected delight. Susanna couldn't very well leave now after accepting the Daubrey's hospitality. Such a thing would be ungracious to say the least. Susanna would make all haste to find a place of her own, lest she become some kind of mushroom, feeding off the kindness of lords and ladies.

"Are..." the maid wetted her lips. "Are you ready to dress for bed now, miss?"

"Yes." Susanna stood. "I think rest is just what I need."

Polly eventually stopped looking at Susanna as if

she suspected she were touched in the head, and helped Susanna dry off and dress in the other chemise she'd brought in her portmanteau.

As Susanna reached for the hairbrush, the maid picked it up. "Allow me, miss."

While Polly brushed and plaited Susanna's hair in one long braid, another maid who looked surprisingly wide-awake appeared and took away the filthy wash water.

Sheepishly, Susanna watched Polly in the mirror. "I'm sorry if you were all awakened to take care of me. I really am accustomed to managing on my own."

"Oh, not to worry, miss. Our days always begin about this time." She sprinkled toothpowder on Susanna's toothbrush and handed it to her.

Susanna brushed her teeth while Polly filled a bed warmer with coals and carried it to the tall four poster bed. How luxurious to have someone care for her and warm her bed!

As Susanna slipped between soft, warm sheets on a mattress like a cloud, she let out a little sigh. "I feel like a new person. Thank you for your help, Polly."

"My pleasure, miss. Sleep well."

The words proved prophetic. Susanna tumbled into a deep slumber. The next time she opened her eyes, late golden rays of afternoon sunlight peeked in between heavy draperies. What a lovely dream. She was warm and safe, and in a beautiful room that reminded her of her childhood bedchamber.

"Miss? Are you awake?" A hushed voice called.

Not a dream, then.

"Miss?" The voice persisted.

"I'm awake," Susanna mumbled.

Polly came into view, peering anxiously at her. "I'm sorry to awaken you, but Lady Daubrey is asking after you."

Susanna pushed herself to a seated position and rubbed her eyes. Then the maid's words sank in. Lady Daubrey. Kit. Susanna was in London in Kit's sister's house—his sister, the titled lady married to a viscount.

"It's four o'clock in the afternoon, miss. You've slept away the whole of the day," Polly said. "Are you ill?"

Groggy, Susanna smiled at Polly. "No, I assure you, I'm quite well. I was merely tired."

"You must have been all worn out, then."

Considering that Susanna hadn't had a proper night's sleep since she left home, that was an understatement. She felt like a new person, content and comfortably drowsy from such a lengthy rest.

"Indeed I was. But I feel much better now."

Polly took a step closer. "I've arranged for the hip bath brought in—unless you want to try the shower bath?"

"The hipbath is perfect, thank you."

Polly rearranged her pillows and placed a tray on her lap. "The bath will be ready in a few minutes, then."

Susanna tried not to gape at the appearance of a tray of food on her lap. While Susanna sat propped by a luxurious number of cushions, she feasted on fruit, scones, and cheese. She washed it down with tea, complete with cream and sugar. How lovely!

After eating, she slipped into the hip bath and scrubbed herself all over again, washing her hair. Once dried and dressed in her clean chemise and the only stays she owned, she slid her arms into a dressing gown Polly held out for her. Fingering the soft dressing gown, she sat at a table while the maid combed and styled her hair.

"Beautiful hair," Polly said.

"It's just brown."

"Oh, no, miss. It's such a rich, dark color and so thick and long. So pretty."

"That's kind of you to say."

Watching through the large, clear mirror, Susanna tried to follow the maid's movements. Over the years, her own poor attempts at styling her hair had resulted in a loose chignon low on the back of her head. Of course her small, dark-spotted and cracked mirror in her bedroom back home had not aided the task. Polly's skilled hands worked too quickly to be a guide for Susanna to recreate later.

Before long, her hair was arranged in a style so becoming that Susanna gaped at her own image. Gone were the unattractive little frizzy pieces that refused to stay smoothed back. Instead, her hair shone smooth and sleek, swept back into an elegant swirl of braids at the crown of her head. Curls framed her face, softening the sharp edges of her features. Why, she almost looked pretty.

A firm knock at the door provided only a second's warning before Esther—Lady Daubrey—swept into the room. All style and elegance and self-possession, she walked as a woman confident with the world and her place in it. Though dressed in a simple muslin gown, she exuded the very finest *ton*, from the excellent cut and workmanship of her gown, to the artful arrangement of her hair, to the healthy glow in her complexion that indicated she'd received ample nourishment all her life. Over her arm she carried pale blue fabric—a gown or a wrap, perhaps.

Kit's sister glided like a queen to Susanna. "You look better, I must say. The dark circles under your eyes are gone. And your skin! Lovely—creamy and flawless like a china doll, and there is color in your cheeks now. And your hair! Oh, I had no idea it was such a beautiful shade." She nodded. "Well done, Polly. The style is perfect for her face."

Polly curtsied and moved to stand near the wall with all the silence of a well-trained servant.

"Thank you," Susanna said. "I apologize for sleeping so late—"

"Think nothing of it. You clearly needed the rest. Did you sleep well?"

"Better than I have in . . . what seems like a long time." She swallowed, ashamed to reveal that she'd only napped on the mail coach when possible but the road conditions made sleep difficult. Then, once in London, she'd spent the night in an alley.

"I brought you a gown to wear while yours are properly laundered. Polly noticed your portmanteau got wet so your other gown was soiled. I'm happy to let you borrow one of mine." She held up a sky blue gown she'd been carrying over her arm.

A gown that fit Esther's full figure surely would not fit Susanna's shapeless frame.

As if guessing her thoughts, Esther added, "It's an apron style gown so I believe it can be pinned in enough to fit you, although it might be too long. Here, try it." She made a quick gesture to the maid.

Polly dashed forward and helped Susanna out of her dressing gown and into the blue gown which opened at the front. After much tucking and pinning, the maid stepped back and glanced at Esther for her approval. Susanna glanced in the mirror. The gown fit her as if made for her, although long enough to drag a little on the floor. Susanna ran a hand along the skirt, savoring the softness of the fine cambric.

"Yes," Esther nodded, circling Susanna. "Yes, I believe that will do." She looked her over critically. "I apologize for giving you an afternoon gown rather than a formal evening gown but it's the only thing I had that I thought might fit you—you're so tiny. We are only having a family dinner tonight, so no need to worry about dressing formally enough for guests."

Still stroking the gown, Susanna let out a tiny sigh of pleasure. "It's lovely, my lady. I don't know how to thank you."

Esther glanced at the maid as if guessing the source of her information but returned her gaze to Susanna. "Oh, let's leave off all this 'my lady' business. Esther suits me much better. Or Tess, as Kit has always called me. And remember, my husband prefers to be called Daubrey. Come, dinner is ready."

Susanna flushed. "I don't think I could be so familiar with a viscount."

"As you wish. But please know that we won't insist on formality while you're here in our home. By the way, I invited Kit to join us for dinner tonight, as well. He visits far too seldom."

Susanna almost laughed at the force of nature that was Esther Daubrey. There was nothing for it but to go along with her. For now. Susanna refused to impose on the Daubreys' hospitality a moment longer than she must. Still, the thought of seeing Kit again sharpened her senses and put a bounce in her step.

Polly brought Susanna silk stockings unlike any Susanna had ever owned, tying the garter above her knee. Her shoes looked shabby and crude by comparison to the fine gown and stockings. Thank goodness for the overly long hem. After adding a pair of blond lace gloves, Susanna was pronounced ready.

Esther linked arms with Susanna. "The gentlemen await us in the drawing room."

As they descended the staircase, Esther kept up a steady stream of conversation about places she wanted to bring Susanna, trips to the theatre for various operas and theatrical productions, and laughing over the habit of many theatre-goers to watch other patrons more than the stage performers.

After crossing the great hall, they reached a set of double doors. Here, Esther paused and fixed a sober gaze on her. Very gently, she said, "I won't ask you prying questions, but it's clear to me that you've suffered recent losses, and I realize you are not in a situation that you have been bred to face. Please know that if I can be of any assistance, you have only to ask. I hope you view me as your friend."

Tears burned the back of Susanna's throat.

"Thank you. You have already been too kind, and I do not wish to impose on your charity."

"It's not charity—it's friendship. This is what friends do. You clearly matter to Kit, therefore you matter to me. Besides, I like you already, and that says something about your character. I usually don't like people I meet in London." She quirked a grin and drew Susanna into the drawing room.

Certainly Esther did not seem the type to be disagreeable. Did she truly mean most people in London were so unlikable? Perhaps she merely jested.

Kit's voice greeted them. "...a brother who was killed in a sea battle, and wants more information about it. Can you help?"

"I'd be happy to look into it for you," came Daubrey's reply.

Her pulse leaped. Did Kit refer to her search for news of Richard? Had he truly remembered?

Inside the doorway, Susanna halted. Kit stood dressed in a black evening suit almost identical in cut and fabric to Lord Daubrey's. Kit's expertly tailored clothing fit his lean, graceful, masculine form. Clearly more than a gifted violinist, Kit carried himself with the same confidence as Lord Daubrey—a man with the world at his feet.

This begged the question; who, really, was Kit Anson?

Kit turned and grinned, his gaze passing over the length of her. Under his scrutiny, her cheeks burned and her steps faltered. She glanced back at the door, her muscles bunching, urging her to flee this auspicious company so far above her in elegance and refinement and town polish. Who was she, a penniless country girl without the training necessary to move in such circles, to think she could pass the evening in their company? They seemed kind enough not to point out all the *faux pas* she would surely commit tonight, but the idea that they must feel obligated to politely bite their tongues as she made one blunder after another was enough to make her wish she'd stayed on the streets. Almost. The bath and the bed had been heavenly. But still...

As if sensing her rising panic, Esther put an arm around her. "You're among friends, my dear." She led her to the gentlemen.

Lord Daubrey eyed her as if he'd never seen her before and had not yet decided what to make of her.

Susanna sank in to a curtsy. "Good evening. Thank you again for your hospitality, my lord."

Lord Daubrey bowed. "Please, I'm Daubrey to my friends."

She inclined her head when she wanted to shake it over the unthinkable position of having a lord imply he was her friend. He'd barely met her and they'd certainly never exchanged more than a few words.

With his whole focus fixed upon Susanna, Kit approached, all grace and poise, and bowed before her. He stared at her as if he saw something wondrous. Which was ridiculous. "Good evening."

Susanna swallowed and sank into a curtsy. How strange to be so formal with Kit. But then, he'd always treated her like a lady, even when she slept in the alley.

"I'm almost speechless with your beauty, Miss Dyer."

She blushed at the astonishment in his expression. "You needn't stare so."

"Indeed I must." He took her hand and raised it to his lips.

Her gloves provided no true barrier between the warmth of his lips and her hand. Heat burst from the contact and spread over her limbs. Heaven help her if he'd kissed her skin directly.

"I must have looked dreadful then, because while I own up to looking better than usual—thanks to your sister and her maid—I am not foolish enough to believe I am anywhere near...beautiful." She choked on the word.

Very gently, and laced with a touch of humor, he said, "I am sorry, but I must disagree."

She must have been truly a dirty ragged little thing then to appear so different to him now. She blushed again and looked down lest she find messages in his eyes that he did not mean to send.

"Dinner is served," the butler announced.

With Lord and Lady Daubrey leading the way, Susanna accepted Kit's offered arm and proceeded to the dining room. Large iron candelabras stood in each corner filled with a dozen candles each, and their light, combined with sconces on the walls and candles on the table, illuminated the elegant room to mid-afternoon brightness. Light shimmered off gilt wood trim, crystal glasses, and fine china adoring the settings.

Lord Daubrey sat at the head of the table with Esther at his right. At Lord Daubrey's left, Kit held out a chair and waited expectantly. Susanna hesitated. She was to sit in a place of honor next to the host? She glanced at Esther, but no one seemed to think seating Susanna in such an honored place anything out of the ordinary. She sat. As Kit took the chair next to her, she glanced around, noticing that their seats were clustered at one end of the table. Kit sent her a reassuring smile. Susanna took a steadying breath. She could do this. Somehow, she would get through the meal without embarrassing Kit or her hosts.

Servants carried out an assortment of dishes, enough for twice as many diners. This was a simple family meal? Susanna called upon her memory about instruction for eating in formal occasions. With trembling hands, she sipped her drink. As the meal began, she watched Esther for cues.

Kit touched her arm. "I spoke with Daubrey about your brother."

"Indeed," Lord Daubrey said, "I'm happy to look into his final hours. What was his name and on which ship did he serve?"

She shot a grateful look at Kit and replied, "His name was Richard Dyer. He was a lieutenant on the HMS *Evening Star* serving under Captain Marshall."

Lord Daubrey nodded. "I will find out what I can."

"I'm very grateful to you, my lord. Er, Daubrey." Susanna glanced at Esther. "I appreciate your hospitality. I will make every effort to secure lodging of my own as soon as possible."

"Nonsense." Lord Daubrey waved his fork. "Stay as long as you like. Esther is thrilled to have a friend staying here."

"I certainly am, and no more talk of imposing or appreciating hospitality, for goodness sake." Esther shook her head. "I told you that I'm looking forward to seeing some of the sights of the city. It's always more fun doing that with someone who's new to town because they enjoy it more than those who've seen it for years. I also want a woman's opinion when I go shopping."

Susanna gave her an apologetic smile. "I'm not sure I could be much help on your shopping

145

selections. I haven't been following London fashions."

Esther waved that away. "Well, if you ask me, many of them are horrid. I mostly need you to help me choose colors and restrain me if I try to put too much lace on something."

Considering the tasteful simplicity of Esther's evening gown, or the beautiful blue creation she'd lent to Susanna, too much lace didn't appear to be a fault.

The second course arrived but Susanna was so full that she could barely sample enough of the delightful dishes to avoid appearing ungracious to the host and hostess. When dessert arrived, she couldn't eat more than a few bites.

Susanna leaned back and let out a contented sigh. How would she ever move? She would never again take for granted the delightful luxury of a full stomach.

"Do you have other plans this evening?" Kit asked Esther and Daubrey.

"Not on the Sabbath," Esther said. She smiled at Susanna. "We usually stay home and read or enjoy music on Sundays."

Oh, dear. She'd completely forgotten today was Sunday and had slept through church. Mama must be shaking her head up in heaven over Susanna's carelessness. Her aunt often denied her the privilege of attending church, but she'd never failed to attend because she'd forgotten. "It sounds relaxing," Susanna said.

"It is indeed," Esther said. "Once the Season starts, it's usually such a whirlwind that we look forward to quiet evenings at home on occasion. Might you favor us with a bit of music, this evening? We have a harp in the music room. The rest of us can perform in our own way as well."

"I'd be happy to play for you, if that is your wish." She rubbed her fingers together, testing their soreness. Her calluses had softened in the preceding week of travel, and the last two nights she'd played a great deal, but no blisters seemed to have formed.

Rather than the ladies leaving and allowing the gentleman to linger over their port, they all rose from the table together. With her arm resting on Kit's, she followed the Daubrey's to the drawing room sectioned off to create a smaller, more intimate setting. Inside sat an ornate harpsichord, a gleaming pianoforte, and a Louis XVI harp with more gilding than even the harpsichord. The first time she'd been in this room, Susanna had been so focused on Kit and his family that she had hardly noticed the furnishings. A fire crackled merrily in the grate and candles flickered from all corners, atop every tabletop, and from crystal chandeliers hanging from the soaring ceilings. The lighting illuminated the room with luxurious brightness.

Esther took a turn at the pianoforte, proving herself a skilled musician. After several numbers, she raised her brows at Kit. "Did you bring your violin?"

"Not tonight, alas." Kit grinned.

"Then you must sing for us instead."

Kit glanced at Susanna. "Will you sing a duet with me?"

"Oh, I don't really have a fine voice. But I look forward to hearing you sing."

Kit made a self-deprecating bow. "I hope I don't disappoint."

As Esther played, Kit sang. He did, indeed have a rich, smooth voice as Susanna had suspected. After a few formal numbers, they led the others in several well-known folk songs. By the end of the evening, they were all standing around the pianoforte singing as a group. The music seemed to bind them together. For a time, Susanna forgot they were anything but the dearest of friends. Indeed, they almost felt like family.

At the end of one of the songs Susanna had been singing gustily, Kit touched the small of her back. "You are overly modest. You have a lovely voice, and I hope to hear you sing more." His eyes shone softly, and his gaze lowered to her lips.

Her mouth dried at the idea that he might be thinking about kissing her. She'd never so badly in all her life wanted to be kissed than she did at that moment.

That would be foolish, for if she kissed Kit, she'd lose another piece of her heart to him, and those pieces would be gone forever when she must say good bye.

He dropped his hand and stepped back. "Will you play for us now?"

"Oh, do!" Esther exclaimed.

Susanna obliged them, playing not as she did for her uncle as a way of escaping her life as a virtual prisoner, but as she once had as a child, to share and please her family. That sensation of belonging, here and now, permeated every inch of her, and her joy wove through her music. How dear Kit and the Daubreys had become to her so quickly!

Each time she finished a piece, they begged for more and more, until finally Esther declared they were probably wearing out their star performer.

Kit arose. "I suppose it is past time that I leave. I bid you all a good night."

Esther stood and kissed his cheek. "I'm so happy you spent the evening with us. Will you come with us as I take Susanna on a little sight-seeing tour of the city tomorrow?"

He glanced at Susanna, a smile tugging on the corners of his mouth. "Yes, I would enjoy that—if that meets with Susanna's approval."

Susanna smiled. "Of course. It would be a pleasure to have you with us."

He came to Susanna and took her hand, enfolding it in both of his. Something intense and searching in his eyes made her pulse pound. Again he raised her hand to his lips. Again came that answering warmth like a candle flame, flickering wider and brighter.

He smiled gently. "Until tomorrow, then."

She swallowed. "Good night."

When he left, she put her hands over her hot cheeks. He most certainly had taken another piece of her heart with him.

Chapter Ten

Kit leaned an arm on the back of Daubrey's barouche and admired Susanna's pretty face and unaffected smile as she gazed at the sights of London. Though she schooled her features so as not to gawk too much like a green girl from the country, the light in her eyes and the awed smile gave away her delight. He grinned at Tess, silently praising her for making sure much of their sightseeing remained inside the carriage so as not to tire out Susanna. After a second night's sleep safe in a bed, as well as several nourishing meals, she looked better than he would have believed. The dark circles under her eyes vanished, her skin virtually glowed, and a new confidence straightened her spine. Even her smiles came more easily now.

All the while, Kit kept a sharp watch for men who might take unusual notice of Susanna. He would not allow a hired thug, or anyone else for that matter, to spirit her away. Clearly, she had more value to her family than she understood. If she were so important to them, why would they starve and neglect her? Each moment he spent in her company chastised him for having once believed her capable of lies or theft, however briefly.

They viewed the Tower of London and then a private museum. Kit divided his attention between watching Susanna enjoy herself and guarding her from harm. With her next to him, he felt a renewed purpose, as if he'd only been dozing the last few years and had finally come fully awake. Colors seemed brighter, scents stronger, sounds richer. With her near, he'd wondered how he'd ever managed the monotony of life. Without his music, he might have faded completely away. But now she was here, and he wanted her near him always. Always. He tasted the word and found it sweet.

Later they drove over London Bridge, and even enjoyed flavored ices at Gunter's. After finishing the last drop of her ice, Susanna turned her gaze upon him and his heart expanded.

With eyes aglow, she asked, "May we visit Wapping and walk along the river?"

She'd remembered. Why that meant so much to him, he couldn't have said, except that it seemed yet another thread in the bond tying him to her.

He almost leaned forward to touch her face. Instead, he gripped the back of the seat. "I noticed it was high tide when we drove over the bridge, so we can't walk on the beach, but there are several shops that have walkways along it that we might visit."

Susanna smiled with such brilliance that his heart did an odd little flip.

"That sounds delightful," Tess said. She gave the instruction to the driver.

Once reaching the area he sought, Kit stepped out and handed down both ladies, tucking their hands in his elbows and glancing sharply about for lurking pick pockets and those seeking to snatch Susanna for a reward or otherwise. In Wapping, the very air felt different—ancient and wise and timeless. They strolled along the edge as far as possible and came up on the watermen's stairs. The water gurgled and sloshed, devouring most of the steps leading downward like some thirsty dog lapping up water.

Susanna watched it as if mesmerized. "This place has such a tremendous sense of history. I almost feel more connected to my heritage as an Englishwoman just by being here amid such a timeless place. This river has surely seen much change over the centuries."

"It has," Kit agreed. "The river itself is so changeable, and yet constant."

Even Tess was subdued. Quietly, she asked, "Shall we explore the other steps? They are all a little unique."

By taciturn agreement, they skirted the edges of warehouses until they came to the narrow passageways between them leading to other steps, some well-kept, others in disrepair, all giving that sense of living timelessness. Ships sailed by as they had for millennia, their wakes stirring up the water even more like breakers on a seashore.

It gave him no small sense of pride to share this with Susanna, knowing that she felt the same respect as he.

Tess finally turned them home, reminding them of tea and the need for Susanna to rest before dinner so she could be fresh for the evening's performance.

Susanna looked up into his eyes, smiling softly. His chest tightened and his whole focus fixed upon her lips. At the moment, the temptation to kiss her almost overcame his gentlemanly restraints. He ached for her, for what he might share with her.

"Thank you for showing this to me," she said.

With all sincerity, he said, "Believe me when I say it was very much my pleasure."

She blushed and looked down but tightened her hold on his arm. He imagined how it would be to take her into his arms in truth and hold her close. He might never let her go.

After returning home, he saw them both inside where they had tea. How comfortable it was to sit here with Tess and Susanna, as if they really were family.

Tess glanced at the clock and stood. "I'm going to rest before dinner. Perhaps you'd like to rest as well, Susanna?"

"Thank you, I believe I would." Susanna said.

Tess nodded and left them alone.

Susanna smiled at Kit. "Thank you so much for a lovely day. And thank you for keeping watch. I noticed how alert you were. Do you think that man my aunt paid to take me back will try to force me back again?"

A fierce protectiveness arose within him. "If that's true, I won't let it happen."

Her smiled turned soft, and a velvety light shone in her gray-blue eyes. "I know. I feel safe with you."

His focus narrowed on her lips. A physical ache swelled up inside him again. But he couldn't. He'd be taking advantage of her as a guest in his sister's home. And he had not yet declared his intentions.

He swallowed. Stepped back. Bowed. "I will return tonight for dinner and to escort you to the theatre."

"I look forward to it." Admiration and even longing shone in her eyes.

He had better proceed slowly with...well, whatever it was that he intended to do. Exhilarated with anticipation, he returned home, changed into his concert attire and all but skipped to the Daubrey's house in time for dinner.

Tess met him at the door. With a lowered voice, she said, "We need to start thinking of Susanna as a respectable lady who is my guest, and not as a girl without a family you brought home from the orchestra."

Kit blinked. "Meaning....?"

"She needs to have a chaperone. You cannot continue to spend time alone with her in a closed coach as you come and go from this house."

"I see." She was right, of course. As a guest of the Daubrey's, Susanna would eventually fall under public scrutiny. Failure to adhere to propriety might reflect poorly on all of them.

Tess continued, "I could chaperone when you go to the theatre this evening, but I will be attending the Earl and Countess Tarrington's dinner party, so I cannot bring you back."

"They're having a dinner party this early? The Season has not yet begun." He only kept track by his rehearsal schedule, which would begin next week for the new opera of the Season.

"This is for the Tarrington's closest friends," Tess explained. "Their ball is not scheduled to take place until the Season officially begins. I must be there tonight and it would be unseemly for me to leave early."

Kit shrugged. "I can take a hackney or walk."

"And leave her alone? No, Kit, that would never do. I have hired a companion to accompany her on your evening excursions to and from the opera house, and during the day when I cannot be with her. The companion will ride with you in the carriage, only—not go with Susanna into the theatre. She begins tonight."

He nodded. "Thank you for protecting her reputation."

Her serious expression lightened. "I have a number of reasons for wishing to do so." She grinned and raised her brows.

Before he could question her regarding that comment, she took him into a sitting room and introduced him to the chaperone, Mrs. Hart, a middle-aged, full-figured lady who sat sewing. Mrs. Hart curtsied but seemed rather dismissively about it as if she'd rather resume her work.

As Kit and Tess returned to the drawing room, he spared a moment to mourn his carefree relationship with Susanna when conventions didn't rule their time together. There would be no more dancing on the lawn. Then again, perhaps it was time to change the nature of their relationship to explore new possibilities.

He felt Susanna's arrival before he turned around. When he did, he almost gaped. She looked even more beautiful than before. Her skin fairly glowed in the candlelight, and her sleek hair shone. True warmth and sincere affection shimmered in her eyes. Most of all, her smile lit up his life, his world, his heart. His breath hitched. She was more than lovely; she was everything good and pure and sincere. During dinner, he could barely manage a polite conversation. The air seemed thick with awareness of her.

As usual before performance, he ate lightly and was gratified to see Susanna consuming more food than she had the previous night. Perhaps her stomach was becoming accustomed to regular feeding. If only he'd found her sooner before she'd been reduced to such straights. It made him want to confront her relatives. With a weapon.

When the time came, Kit pushed back his chair. "I wish we could linger, Tess, but we need to get to the theatre."

"I have a carriage ready to take you," Esther said. "I'll send another one to pick you up tonight, Susanna."

Susanna stammered, "That's very kind but really—"

"I won't hear of you walking to and from the theatre," Esther said. "I know Kit fancies himself a knight errant who can defend you from all the ruffians that prowl the streets at night, but a lady need not walk so far at such an hour—it's cold and damp."

"She's right," Daubrey said.

As Susanna stood, her smile turned pained as if

inwardly she was writhing. "Thank you again. Good night." She curtsied to them and took Kit's arm.

"Oh, wait," Esther called. "I have a pelisse that will be lovely with that frock and it will be warmer than yours. You'll take that." Her tone allowed no room for argument. She made a quick gesture to a liveried footman.

The footman stepped up with a cobalt-blue velvet pelisse at that moment. He handed it to Kit. He draped it around her, pausing a moment to touch her shoulders. The footman also handed her a pair of kid gloves.

Susanna ran her fingers over them. "So soft. Almost like satin."

Her smile looked wistful.

Tess called, "Mrs. Hart, they are ready." She smiled at Susanna. "The chaperone I told you about is ready to accompany you."

Susanna's brow furrowed. "But I assured you, she isn't necessary."

Kit put a hand on her arm. "I know our meeting took place under unusual circumstances. In fact, our entire relationship has taken place under unusual circumstances. Even though you and I have already traveled together in a closed coach, Esther and I agree it's best if you have a chaperone now."

"I appreciate the sentiment, but I belong to the

working class now, and I have been alone for long enough that such measures are probably a moot point."

Poor Susanna. No gently bred lady should endure all the indignities she had suffered. "Be that as it may, you are a guest of my sister's so it would be best if we followed conventions."

She cast a panicked look at the door as if considering running.

"What is it?" he said.

She let out a huff and looked down. "It's just that..." she glanced at Tess. "Forgive me, I appreciate everything you have done, and are doing, but I have lived so long under my aunt's control that I..." She shrugged. "It's nothing. This is your home, and of course you must do what you think is best."

Tess bit her lip. "Forgive me, I did not intend to make you feel as if you have no say. I only had your best interest at heart. I suppose I can be overbearing at times."

Susanna smiled, but it came out looking almost pained. "I understand."

Kit exchanged glances with Tess. They should not have been so heavy handed with her. Just because she stayed here didn't mean they had the right to manage her life. She surely must have enjoyed her taste of freedom just as Kit had when he left home.

Mrs. Hart appeared carrying a bag. Some kind of knitted cloth peeped out the top. While Tess made the introductions, the chaperone and Susanna nodded to one another. Mrs. Hart walked out ahead of them and got into the coach.

As they stepped outside, Kit glanced at Susanna's strained features. "We didn't intend to make you feel as if you have no say over your decisions."

She lifted her shoulder. "Your sister is very thoughtful and generous. I should be more grateful." Her words fell flat.

"She can be a bit of a bully, too," Kit said. "And, apparently, so can I. You most assuredly do not need to be more grateful. We ought to be more sensitive to your wishes. Tess is still sulking over not having a sister, so she'll surely subject you to all manner of fussing. You'll need to put your foot down. I apologize for not consulting your feelings on the matter."

She glanced at him from underneath her lashes. "You should apologize for omitting that she had married a viscount."

He waved that off. "Don't make more of it than there is. Besides, she's only my sister, and Daubrey is just my brother's friend from school who spent summers and holidays with us."

She stopped on the front step and lowered her voice, probably so the chaperone wouldn't overhear. "I don't belong here with them."

He put a hand on either side of her shoulders, turning her toward him. "Believe me when I say that you fit right in."

"If my parents had lived and I'd had the benefit of my mother's tutelage, dance masters, French teachers, a governess, and perhaps a few London seasons to develop some Town polish, I might have belonged to this world. Not now. Probably not ever. I'm too backwards and unsophisticated."

With a finger under her chin, he lifted her face upward to his. "Susanna Dyer, you are poised and gracious and well mannered. You carry yourself as a lady no matter your circumstances. You belong in their world as much as they." He waited until the misery faded from her eyes.

A little curving of her lips assured him that his words had not completely fallen by the wayside. Kit led her to a waiting coach and he handed them in. With the chaperone present, speech halted. As they traveled, Kit wrestled with the magnitude of Susanna's statement about her sensibilities and that she'd become jaded. What, exactly, did that mean? Had some harm come to her as she slept in the streets? Torn between asking probing questions that were none of his business, and fearing the answer should she confide in him, he sat gripping his violin case as if it were in danger of suddenly leaping out of his hands.

162

The idea that such a gentle soul had fallen on such hard times tugged at his heart. The thought of her falling prey to unscrupulous characters turned his insides out.

He'd initially felt a pull toward her because she'd been a damsel in distress. Later, her gift as a musician had drawn him to her. There was something else about her that captured his interest, some connection he could not hope to understand without years of exploring it, which sounded more appealing every moment.

Susanna shot darting glances at him with eyes that glittered in the occasional glow of lamplights they passed. If she'd suffered indignities and abuses, she might very well be afraid of men. At first, he viewed her behavior as extreme reticence but now it seemed to be true wariness. If only he'd learned sooner she'd had nowhere to sleep!

She remained silent until they reached the stage entrance. As he handed her out of the carriage, he kept a grip on her hand. She looked up at him with an inquiry in her eyes. A dozen questions ran through his mind, but nothing seemed appropriate.

She glanced at the companion, the silent Mrs. Hart, and said, "Thank you Mrs. Hart."

The older woman inclined her head. "I will return with the carriage later tonight, Miss."

As Kit escorted her to the back stage entrance, he moistened his lips. "I won't ask you prying questions, but please know that you can confide in me if you ever feel the need to unburden yourself."

In a small voice, she said, "Thank you."

He tightened his grip. "I mean that. I'll help you any way I can."

She looked into his eyes with such a deep probing that he remained still, letting her look her fill and see the truth of his words. Instead, her own sincerity revealed itself. She was as guileless as a child. How could he have thought her guilty of theft or of playing a role two days past? The idea shamed him.

His attention focused on her lips. Were they as soft and sweet as they appeared? Again came that pull, this time as a woman beckons a man. Before he lost his head and did something to besmirch her reputation, he stepped back.

Inside the orchestra pit, she shed her wrap and gloves. She ran a hand along the fabric of her borrowed gown as if she'd never worn anything so fine. It certainly was a sight better than the rags she wore when he met her. After greeting the only other two female musicians, she settled in to warm up and tune. The other two female musicians exclaimed over her change in appearance but her response got lost in the pre-concert raucous.

Kit realized he was staring. He focused his thoughts and began his usual pre-performance routine of tuning, warm ups, and quieting his mind. The performance went. Nothing noteworthy happened except for the sense of wholeness he once again experienced during his violin-harp duet. He could have played that passage all night.

At the conclusion, Alex gestured at Kit. "I got word today that our regular harpist is returning tomorrow, so please tell your little ladybird that she is no longer needed. The manager will have her wages ready in the morning. She needs to go see him in his office."

Closing his eyes, Kit let out his breath slowly. Poor Susanna. She'd be crushed. Now what? "I'll tell her. But she's a lady—not a ladybird."

Kit glanced at Susanna. She stood chatting with the only female musicians, smiling and eyes alight as if all were right with the world. How could he ruin that?

After wiping and packing his violin, he donned the careless façade he once wore when he played the society games in an effort to please his family before he walked away from what his father called the "duties of his class" and found his own place in the world. Of course, that place had grown somewhat lonely of late. Truth be told, he missed his family. Seeing both his

165

mother and his sister in the same week reminded him how much they meant to him. Perhaps he ought to make a point to pay a call on his brother, Dunlap, when he arrived in London. Just because they disagreed on, well, almost everything, didn't mean they should cut all ties of communication.

Kit strolled to Susanna and smiled politely at the other two women.

"Evening, Mr. Anson." The younger of the pair grinned. "You and Susanna fairly brought the house down again tonight with your duet. You are quite a pair."

He glanced at Susanna. "It's a pleasure to play with such a talented and passionate musician." Was she as passionate in other areas? He wanted to find out.

She had become a friend, a kindred spirit. She also had the refined manners of a princess, without the haughtiness. His mother would probably like her. If Susanna got over her overly abundant gratitude, she would fit in nicely with his family and their circle of friends—the intimate ones, at least. His father, of course, would find her beneath the family standards and would never accept her, but Kit never saw the old tyrant anyway.

He held out an arm to Susanna. "I'll see you back now, if you wish."

Smiling, she took his arm. "After you drop me off, are you having dinner at the Silver Duck as usual?"

"Esther invited me to stay for a late meal when I deliver you home."

Did he imagine her pleasure? In the orchestra pit's dim lighting, he could not be certain if she were blushing and if her downward gaze hid a sparkle.

The Daubrey's carriage awaited them and Kit handed Susanna in. They greeted Mrs. Hart who nodded, yawned, and looked outside again.

Susanna let out a happy sigh. "If I had known how much pleasure I could derive from performing in front of a live audience, I would have done this sooner. How long do you think I have this position?"

A direct question, needing a direct response. He let out his breath, finding his courage to tell her the bad news. "In truth, I just learned that the other harpist plans to return tomorrow night.

"So soon?" Her posture deflated. In a small voice, she said, "It's good that his injury was not so severe, then." She swallowed.

"The manager will have your wages ready for you on the morrow," he added.

She nodded, her brow furrowed. "I need to find another position, and quickly."

"There are other orchestras. Vauxhall Gardens, the Royal Orchestra, and there are always small groups who hire themselves out for dinner parties and balls and such. I will write you a letter of recommendation, and Alex will, I am sure. I will do anything I can to help you."

She gave him a pained smile. "Thank you, but you've already done too much. I am beholden to you beyond my ability to repay you—and Esther, as well."

"I don't want repayment, and you know it. As I told you, I was once a musician with virtually nothing."

She fixed a steady pair of eyes on him. "You've never had nothing. You have parents, a brother, and a sister who clearly loves you. You were only alone because you chose to be."

Her words struck him. She was right, of course. He had been driven to prove to his father, and himself, that he could succeed on his own merit. He had also felt moral-bound to reject his father's method of making money. If he were honest, he also had been delighted to leave behind all the silly pretenses and pretty lies found in the ballrooms of the upper crust of society. However, he'd never gone truly hungry. He had never slept in an alley. If his situation had grown desperate, all he had to do was swallow his pride and access his allowance, or even go home.

He nodded to concede her point. "Be that as it may, I once had uncertain prospects and missed a few meals. Alex gave me a chance. I cannot repay him directly but I would be ungrateful if I didn't help you."

She nodded, studying her fingers. "I appreciate your sense of duty."

Perhaps he had helped her out of duty at first—the same way he would have helped an old woman who'd fallen in the street. Now, his motivation for helping Susanna had become different. He liked her. He liked spending time in her company. The night they had talked and danced had been one of the most enjoyable nights of his life, as had each moment he spent in her company from the very first moment. When the lawman had made a grab for her, a surprisingly protective side of him had come out. Yet that protective side is not what drove him to see her safely settled with a position and a place to live—not to mention that something needed to be done about the charges against her or she'd never be safe.

Still, none of that explained why he wanted so badly to see her happy nor why he thought of her all his waking hours or why thoughts of touching her became all-consuming. It all centered around her, and his ever-growing feelings for her.

Was this love?

They arrived at Daubrey's house. His sister greeted them as they arrived. "How did the performance go?"

Kit handed his coat and hat to the butler. "Brilliantly, as usual."

Susanna removed her pelisse and said quietly, "The principal harpist is returning tomorrow so they won't be needing me anymore."

Tess glanced at Kit. He nodded. She put her arm around Susanna. "Not to worry, my friend."

Susanna's mouth pulled into a tight smile. "With the money I've earned so far, I ought to be able to rent a room from a boarding house. Would you write me a letter of introduction?"

Tess squeezed her shoulder. "I could, of course, but then I would be robbed of the privilege of enjoying your company. Won't you please stay? We can visit museums and shop to our heart's content, and won't have to worry about hurrying home so you can rest before your performance."

Good ol' Tess, always turning bad news into good.

Susanna smiled sadly. "I cannot remain here on your charity indefinitely. I only came because I'd believed it was temporary—that I could be independent in the near future."

"All the more reason for you to stay. I certainly won't stand by and allow you to go when you have nowhere to live." Tess softened her voice, turned pleading. "Please stay as my guest. Tomorrow if the weather is fine, I want to take you riding at the park."

Susanna faltered. "That's very kind of you, but I don't have a riding habit, and I haven't been on a horse in years."

"No riding then," Tess said. "We'll go to the exhibition at the Royal Academy of Art and do some of those other activities I've been excited to share with you. Today our sightseeing gave me a taste of what diversions we can have together."

Susanna shook her head. "I cannot spare the time. I must search for a new position, learn if there are any scheduled auditions." She glanced at Kit. "I don't suppose next time I can simply show up at a stage door and beg every concertmaster to arrange an impromptu audition."

Kit said, "I will make inquiries for you and write you a letter of recommendation as I'm sure Alex will."

Susanna hesitated.

"No need to decide tonight," Tess said. "You both need food. It's been hours since dinner, and neither of you ate much then."

Tess led them into the dining room where footmen carried in platters of bread, cheese, soup, and fruit. Kit tucked into his meal but Susanna only picked at her food. How could he alleviate her fears? Surely she knew Tess and Daubrey would give her a home and food for as long as she needed it. Her reluctance to accept charity was admirable but misplaced in this instance. Although he had to admit, she reminded him a great deal of himself when he first left home, determined to prove to himself and his father that he had the strength and tenacity to manage his own affairs and be independent. If only he could smooth the worry lines from her face. He would set about sending messages to everyone he knew in the music world to help find her a position. Of course, there was another way to see to her financial needs...

Daubrey entered, greeted everyone, and took a seat next to Susanna. "Miss Dyer, I made some inquiries for you and have learned that your brother's captain is in town. I took the liberty of sending him a message requesting his presence. He replied that he'd be delighted to speak with you tomorrow morning, if that suits you."

Susanna's eyes lit up. "Oh, that would be lovely, thank you."

Tess interjected. "We'll visit the museum afterwards."

"I also wish to meet with the theatre manager," Susanna said. "He will have my pay ready."

"Of course," Tess agreed.

Kit glanced at Susanna, toying with the offer to be present to lend his support while Susanna spoke with the captain about her brother, but held his tongue. Such a meeting would surely be personal, and unless Susanna invited him, it wasn't his place to intrude.

Kit smiled as Tess coaxed Susanna to talk about playing the harp, when she started, what she loved best about it. Susanna's guard dropped as she painted a picture of a country manor. She'd clearly been raised the daughter of a gentleman. If her parents still lived, her life would have been drastically different. Again came that longing to have a few moments alone with the aunt and uncle who should have loved and cared for her.

Susanna and Tess conversed as easily as if they'd been friends for years, even sisters. Perhaps Kit could provide Tess with the sister she'd always wanted. He'd never considered such before meeting Susanna. But the prospect sent energy through him.

He glanced at Susanna whose eyes and posture drooped. "You look weary." He stood. "Thank you for the meal, Tess." As he turned toward the door, a suddenly strong reluctance to leave Susanna halted his steps. He glanced at her. "Would you see me out, please?"

Her brows arched in surprise but she stood and walked with him toward the door. As they crossed the foyer, he took her hand and tried to come up with something to say, some reason to prolong his visit. Her ungloved hand fit into his, so small and delicate.

173

Its warmth spread up his arm and warmed him all over.

He rubbed the back of her hand with his thumb. "Esther clearly loves having you here. Please try not to worry. I'm confident you will secure a new position soon enough."

Her features relaxed. "I do not know what I did to deserve such kindness. I am grateful, nonetheless." She looked up into his eyes, her face glowing with warmth and even affection. "How can I ever thank you?"

When was the last time a female looked at him with such unreserved fondness? Her guileless charm, her sweet, unspoiled honesty touched his heart. How refreshing to be admired by a lady who wanted nothing in return. Her lips parted innocently and curved. A skilled seductress could not have been more tempting than her sincerity.

He leaned in, aching to kiss those lips. He caught himself. If he kissed her now, she might suspect she owed him her favor because he and his sister had helped her. No, he'd wait until she knew his actions sprang from true affection. Instead, he pressed his lips to the back of her hand.

"No need to thank me. I am delighted to be of assistance. If I fail to rescue a lady in need at least once a week, I feel that I am neglectful as a gentleman." He grinned and tapped the tip of her nose. "I hope your meeting with the captain goes well tomorrow." As much as he wanted to be there for her during that meeting, he must respect her privacy, and she had not invited him to join them.

"Thank you." Again came that shy, affectionate glance.

He bowed and stepped out into the night. Whistling all the way home, he hardly noticed the chilly night air. Susanna's face, the sound of her voice, the feel of her hand in his, occupied his thoughts and happily robbed him of sleep until the wee hours of the night.

Chapter Eleven

Standing in the middle of Esther's parlor, Susanna held out her hands, trying to ward off the force of a determined Esther. "I cannot take this from you."

Esther took her by the hand and led her to a low stepstool. "Of course you can. It doesn't fit you as it should, though." The seamstress held the dark blue pelisse while Susanna slid her arms into the sleeves. The seamstress stood back to survey the fit, then sprang into action, measuring and pinning.

Susanna ran a hand over the soft fabric. "If you have it altered, it will no longer fit you."

"It already doesn't fit me." Esther stopped in front of a mirror and smoothed her hair. "I've gained a few stones since I had that made. I have two new ones now, so I have no need of it." She turned and smiled ruefully. "Besides, I am exceedingly vain, and I don't want to be seen with anyone who wears a coat as old as yours. Naturally I think my own taste is best so I will dress you up like the little sister I never had."

Susanna flushed and bit her lip. "I don't suppose I can blame you. I can see how my clothing might be an embarrassment to someone like you."

"Oh, no, I've done it again," Esther said. "I didn't mean that as unkindly as it sounded. You couldn't be an embarrassment even if you tried." She drew nearer and smiled. "You have to admit, though, your coat looks as if it's at least two decades old."

"I cannot argue with that, but—"

Esther held up her hand. "You may have noticed that I am also insufferably spoiled so you might as well give in. I always have my way—it comes from being the only girl in a household of boys, and having a doting husband who cannot refuse my every whim."

Once the seamstress finished, Esther handed Susanna two gowns, one of white cambric and the other pink silk. "Fit these to her, as well."

"Oh, no, really," Susanna said. "This is too much."

"Now, now, none of that." Esther said. "We are having a few friends for dinner tonight. Naturally, as my guest, you will join me. You must have something suitable to wear, and I was planning on giving them away anyway. Tomorrow, we can order some gowns of your own."

Susanna opened her mouth to speak but Esther rushed on. "No objections about the cost. I assure you, it is a trifle. I already spoke with my husband and he assures me that I have not yet spent my dress allowance for this Season. He's so generous with that sort of thing. We are happy to share with you."

Firmly, Susanna said, "No, Esther. I am sorry. I do not mean to insult you or be ungracious about your gifts, but I really cannot allow you to buy new gowns for me for which I have no hope of repaying."

"You are already repaying me by being my friend. You see, I have many acquaintances, and some false friends who only pretend to like me because they are social climbers, or because they want me to introduce them to my older brothers. You clearly don't want anything from me. Naturally, I trust you." She smiled. "Besides, Kit likes you, and I've always trusted his judgement." She sat and picked up a copy of *Ackerman's Repository* and thumbed through the magazine, pausing at the fashion engravings.

Susanna fell silent. She'd never considered ladies in Esther's position might be lonely, without true friends. Perhaps they had more in common than Susanna had first thought.

"I have a proposal," Esther said. "I do not wish to step on your pride or your desire for independence. Allow me to give you the gift of one new gown—only one. Anything else you need can be fitted to you from my last year's wardrobe which I am planning to discard. Please?" She held up her fingers as if measuring something. "Just one teeny little new gown?"

Susanna heaved a sigh. How could she refuse? How could she accept?

Esther stood and came to Susanna, taking her by the hand. "Imagine if our situations were reversed. You would want to do the same, would you not? Wouldn't it give you great pleasure to dress me up?" She gave her a beseeching smile.

Esther was right. If Susanna had the means to help someone with nothing, she certainly would want to go about it just as Esther was for her. Susanna's resistance crumbled.

She spread her hands. "As you wish."

Her new friend smiled triumphantly and clasped her hands together as if she had been given a gift, rather than the other way around.

When the seamstress finished her measurements, promising to have the alterations completed before dinner, Susanna turned her attention upon bathing and enjoying the luxury of having her hair styled again. After dressing in an apron-style gown similar to the one she'd borrowed yesterday, only this one of palest pink, she joined Esther in the parlor to await the captain's visit. Dressed like a true lady, and in the company of her dear new friend, Susanna felt rather like Cinderella at a ball. With any luck, the magic wouldn't end at the stroke of midnight.

In the parlor, she helped Esther sew beads onto a reticule while they chatted like old friends. Underneath it all, her nerves jumped as she

179

anticipated the upcoming interview with her brother's captain. Still, Esther's charm and humor had her relaxing enough to share some girlish giggles.

A servant announced Captain Marshall. Susanna's stomach flipped in all directions as she and Esther stood.

"Thank you for coming, Captain," Esther said to the gentleman.

Captain Marshall bowed. With dark hair shot through with a few strands of silver and the craggy lines on his face of a sea captain, he looked like he might be anywhere from thirty to fifty, and was handsome in a comforting, fatherly sort of way. "I'm happy to be of assistance, Lady Daubrey."

After Esther made the introductions and excused Lord Daubrey's absence due to business, they sat. Susanna smoothed the skirt of her borrowed gown with trembling hands. She spared a grateful thought that she could receive this distinguished captain in a proper gown instead of the threadbare frock she'd worn before becoming the recipient of Esther's generosity.

Captain Marshal addressed Susanna. "I understand you seek information about your brother, Miss Dyer."

This was it—the moment she'd been anticipating. Her pulse leaped about like a crazed dancer. "Yes, sir.

I received your letter, and I thank you for that. In addition, I was hoping you might fill me in on the details."

He nodded. "It's been my experience that people often harbor a hope that there has been some mistake regarding the death of the loved ones. Let me assure you that there is no doubt as to his fate; I identified his body and was present during your brother's burial at sea."

The news, though not unexpected, still hit her with such finality that her eyes burned. She nodded and stared at her hands. When she could speak, she managed, "I hadn't really hoped otherwise. Not really." Her voice broke. He was lost, then. Well and truly lost to her. Blinking and swallowing, she struggled to regain her composure.

Captain Marshall's voice quieted. "He was a fine officer. I had just promoted him to the rank of second lieutenant, and he served with valor."

She nodded again, still too emotional to speak.

Captain Marshall spoke in soothing tones. "He spoke of you often. When he received news of your parent's death, he wrestled between the desire to return home to you, and his commitment to his duty as an officer. His choice to remain in the navy stemmed from his desire to protect his country—and his sister—from Napoleon's dominion."

Pity he hadn't chosen to protect her from her aunt's dominion! Still, she could not begrudge his desire to serve king and country.

She nodded. "I understand."

"What you may not know is that only days before his last battle, he'd had a change of heart and had decided to return home to take his place as head of the household and care for you. I regret that he was unable to do so."

She lifted her head. "He had?"

"Indeed. He had made that desire known to me."

If only Richard had come home sooner, he would still be alive. They could have shared their grief over their parents' death and created happy new memories together. Susanna would have been spared from living under her Aunt Uriana's tyranny—she'd grown so much worse after news of her Richard's death, probably because she no longer had any fear of censure.

Susanna crushed her handkerchief. "How...how did it happen? You said in your letter that it was during a sea battle, but if you know anything more..." She swallowed.

"He was below deck calling instructions to the gunners. We were hit broadside. Water started pouring in through the breach in the hull. Though he was wounded, he carried several of his injured shipmates to safety, and then waded back in to the flooded deck to help board up the hole until the carpenters could perform repairs. The exertion may have aggravated his injuries. He perished a short time later." He paused. "He was a hero, Miss Dyer, and he served king and country with honor."

She nodded and wiped tears running down her face. Esther took her hand and held it. Silently, the captain and Esther waited. There seemed nothing else to say.

Susanna straightened and offered the captain a watery smile. "I thank you for seeing me, Captain. I am grateful to you."

"I am happy to be of assistance. Please accept my condolences."

After bidding the captain goodbye, Susanna went to her bedchamber and splashed water on her face. She stood bracing her hands on either side of the washbasin. What had she hoped to hear? That Richard was only missing and that he might someday come home? War took the lives of countless other brothers, fathers, sons, and husbands. Why should she believe she would be spared?

Esther entered and sat on an armchair drawn up to a small round table. "Would you like to talk about it?"

Susanna shook her head and reached for a towel

to dry her face. Surely if she shared the feelings in her heart, she'd break down and sob all day. She pressed the towel over her face and took several deep breaths.

Esther studied her soberly. "If you aren't feeling quite the thing, we can forego our visit to the museum."

"No, that's not necessary. I suspect a diverting outing is exactly what I need."

Despite her brave words, the last thing she wanted to do was put on a smile and pretend to enjoy herself. Still, she was a guest out of Esther and Daubrey's charity. She owed it to her kind hostess to follow through on their plans.

Esther smiled gently and gestured to the bed where some clothing lay. "I see the alterations for your spencer and pelisse are completed."

Susanna nodded and moved to the bed as Esther held up the spencer so Susanna could slip her arms into the short, jacket-like garment. After fastening the mother-of-pearl buttons, Susanna faced Esther to get her opinion.

"Lovely. I do adore you in blue. It brings out the color of your eyes, and that spencer dresses up that plain apron-style gown nicely. You really have such a lovely complexion." She helped Susanna into the plum-colored pelisse and donned one of her own. "Ready?"

They left the house together. Despite the gloom in Susanna's heart, she cheered after only moments in Esther's exuberant company. They visited the British Museum where Esther acted as an informative tour guide. Later, they strolled along Wapping. Finding that it was low tide, they descended down the waterman's steps and explored the beach of the Thames. Other people scavenged for coal and other items that washed up—among them an old cup, a broken tea pot, several bottles, and even a battered shoe.

Remembering the man who'd tried to seize her, Susanna glanced about. This would be a terrible place for him to find her. She was exposed along the water. He could easily leap out from one of the buildings, snatch her, and spirit her away. She cast a glance at the coachman and footman waiting on the road. Would they lend a hand if she were in danger?

"Oh, and I simply must have some new perfume." Esther's announcement broke into her thoughts. "Shall we return to the coach, or do you wish to remain longer?

"I'm ready to return." Hopefully, Susanna didn't sound too eager.

Still glancing about, Susanna gratefully returned with her friend to the coach. Inside the perfumer, the combination of scents created a chaotically delightful bouquet—everything from fruits such as apples and oranges, to spices like cinnamon and vanilla and bergamot, to flowers, some of which were labeled with names she had never heard of nor could she identify by their smell.

"As a rule, I like undertones of lavender," Esther said. "I want something else to liven up my usual scent. I'm not sure about the blend I want."

As Esther agonized over the types and proportions of scents, aided by a perfumer, a grandfatherly sort of man, Susanna handed her a bottle. "Perhaps you could add a little cinnamon to brighten it."

Esther sniffed and smiled. "Yes, that's better. I'll take one with this combination," she said to the perfumer. "And something else...something...new. What do you like, Susanna?"

They experimented until they finally settled on a blend of gardenia, vanilla, and sweet orange.

Esther took a whiff. "It fits you perfectly."

"Me?" Susanna shook her head. "Oh, no. We are in search of a new fragrance for you."

"This your fragrance—exotic, yet soft."

Susanna almost laughed out loud. She'd never considered a country bumpkin exotic. If only Kit viewed her that way, maybe he'd think of her as a woman instead of a pathetic child in need of rescue.

Oh dear. She was quickly losing her heart to him. While he'd always been so kind and attentive, she had no reason to believe he had any true feelings for her. Why would he? Years of her aunt telling her she was stupid and backward and ugly had eaten away at Susanna's confidence until she had little left. What if her aunt were right? Perhaps they would have loved her and treated her like a member of the family if she had been pretty and graceful and accomplished in something—anything—other than the harp.

"My friend will take one of this blend in a throwaway," Esther said, "and she's not going to argue with me about a little gift such as this." Esther shot Susanna a stern look and addressed the patient perfumer.

Susanna opened her mouth and snapped it shut. Meekly, she said, "Thank you."

Smiling triumphantly, Esther paid for their purchases while a shop girl poured the customized perfumes into tiny scent bottles and put stoppers on the ends.

Susanna fingered the glass cylindrical bottle decorated with hand-painted gilt. "These are called throwaways?"

Esther smiled. "I don't know if everyone throws them away, but their rounded bottoms make it impossible to stand them up, and they tend to roll all over the dresser, so once the perfume is gone, most people discard them. If you like the blend you've customized, we'll come back and buy a larger bottle of it."

Susanna wouldn't dream of asking Esther to buy a large bottle of expensive perfume but she nodded anyway. At Esther's urging, Susanna opened the cork stopper on her sample and dabbed a little behind her ears as she had seen her mother do years ago.

Back inside the carriage, Esther stuck her feet out and pointed, then flexed her toes. "Are your feet as tired as mine?"

"A bit. It's been a truly diverting afternoon." Susanna let out a happy sigh. What a dear friend she'd found in Esther.

"Tea is in order, I believe. And then the dressmaker is coming to measure you and bring samples for gowns of your own."

"Esther, please, I really cannot—"

"Now, now, we've been through this. No arguing. You agreed to one gown and I'm holding you to that." Esther put her arm around Susanna. "I consider you a true friend. You are the sweetest, most unspoiled and delightful young lady I have ever had the privilege of knowing, and I can't wait to show you off at my dinner party tonight."

"I cannot imagine how I will manage a formal dinner party."

"You will manage it as beautifully as you manage our family dinners. Your manners are impeccable, and you're as fresh as a spring flower. Trust me, our guests will love you. Most of all, I expect my brother will once again be unable to keep his eyes off you."

Susanna stared unseeing out of the window, reliving the exhilaration of having Kit so near. The way he'd touched her hand had left her giddy and sleepless most of the night. She quashed that thought.

"He is merely being gallant," Susanna said. "I am a dull country miss with no hope of making a match with a fine gentleman."

"You underestimate your appeal, my dear." Esther smiled smugly.

Susanna only shook her head.

After arriving home and enjoying tea, fruit, and cakes, Susanna barely resisted rubbing her stomach in contentment. "I suspect you are trying to fatten me."

"I am. You are far too thin. If you put on a little weight, your figure will fill out."

Before Susanna had time to be embarrassed about the reminder of her lack of womanly charms, Esther added in a quiet voice, "You clearly haven't eaten enough food on a regular basis in far too long."

Susanna shrugged and looked away. Discussing such unhappy years served no purpose.

Gentle and concerned, Esther said, "You left because they were starving you?"

Susanna picked up a pillow decorated with needlepoint and hugged it. "I left because my aunt was insistent that I marry her nephew, Algernon."

Esther's mouth flattened. "What did she do, tie you to the bedpost and whip you until you agreed?"

"No, she threatened to lock me in my bedchamber until the wedding day."

Esther let out an indignant huff. "Your aunt sounds like a selfish beast. I vow if I ever cross paths with her, I will cut her dead!"

Warmth and friendship trickled over Susanna, and she opened to it like a flower opens to a gentle summer rain. Notwithstanding her concern with how she might find employment and repay Esther—not to mention the underlying fear over the man who was after his reward money finding her again—these were some of the happiest days of her adult life.

Esther let out her breath in disgust. "So that's why you left?"

"That, and because her son...." Heat roared through Susanna at the memory of Percy's indecent proposal. Her brain shouted at her to be silent, but she couldn't seem to make herself stop divulging the shameful truth. "Her son, Percy, wanted me for... something less respectable. I feared he would...." She relived those terrifying moments when she feared he'd burst into her bedchamber. "I feared he would not respect my refusal."

"Good heavens," Esther said indignantly. "I'm almost of a mind to have Kit call out that bounder."

The thought of Kit risking his life to face Percy with swords or pistols left her cold. "I don't want Kit to endanger himself in a duel."

"No, of course not, but that bully must be dealt with." Esther let out another breath of frustration. "So that's why you left so suddenly?"

Susanna nodded. "I'd hoped to secure employment as a harpist. It's my only real skill."

A servant arrived. "The modiste is here, milady."

Esther stood. "Ah, excellent. Show them to my boudoir in a minute. We'll go there now."

Inside a sitting room decorated in gold and red, Esther pulled a low stool out to the middle of the floor. "When the time comes to measure you, you can stand on this. We'll pick out styles first."

The modiste and a young assistant arrived with boxes of samples and fashion engravings. While the woman measured her, Esther helped her select an evening gown in the most glorious shade of rose. She also provided a new chemise of soft linen that made Susanna's look dingy and ragged by comparison.

As the modiste and her assistant gathered up their supplies, a corsetiere arrived with long stays to fit to Susanna. Blushing clear down to her toenails, Susanna stripped down to her chemise and tried on the new, stiff stays. Unlike the short stays she had always worn, which laced up the front, the long stays laced down the back. A flat, hard, wooden busk, or boning, about the width of her two fingers, ran right down the middle between her breasts to separate them.

As the corsetiere pinned to make adjustments, Esther broke in, instructing the corsetiere, "Don't cut off the areas that need to be taken in—leave enough room in the seams to let them out as she puts on weight. I will ensure she isn't this thin for long."

Susanna longed to have the curves of a woman but doubted such a miracle existed. With an embarrassed giggle, she gestured to her bust line. "I probably won't gain weight...here."

"Trust me, you will." Esther smiled like a woman with secrets. "Besides, Kit doesn't seem to mind your figure as it is."

Was it true? Did Kit truly not mind her diminutive figure? With a glance at the corsetiere who must have heard every word, Susanna blushed so hard she feared she'd heat the entire room.

The corsetiere's expression never changed. Perhaps she'd grown accustomed to such talk. She spoke before Susanna could reply. "All done, miss. I'll have these adjustments done in no time."

"Do stay and complete the modifications on the

stays here," Esther said. "We need them in time for a dinner party tonight."

"Yes, milady. Where can I work?" asked the corsetiere.

"Have the nearest footman show you belowstairs."

Susanna would never have imagined being such a powerful lady that a shop keeper would come to her instead of needing to go shopping.

Three hours later, Susanna, refreshed after a nap and a bath, dressed. The crisp new fabric and the different style of her new long stays certainly enhanced her diminutive figure—far better than her old short stays. The center boning and the longer, stiffened fabric felt strange, and she required Polly to lace up the back, but she couldn't deny the improvement to her figure. It also supported her back. Of course, she'd need to keep her short stays for the eventuality that she would need to dress without the aid of a maid.

Dressed in a cream silk gown that had been made over for her, her hair coiffed, and wearing her new perfume, Susanna glided downstairs to the drawing room. Kit caught her eye. He turned, and blinked, then gazed at her as if he'd never seen a more beautiful sight. As heat rushed through her, she smiled while her heart did a dozen crazy little flips.

For tonight, she would forget her past. She would not worry about finding employment. And she most certainly would not allow fears of her relatives or the man they'd sent after her to dim her enjoyment. Tonight, she would bask in the happy warmth of being in Kit's company.

With a wistful sigh, she memorized the beauty of his features. Surely, she would not be allowed to admire them much longer. Still, she'd enjoy them while she could and tuck them away with her other Sweet Memories.

Chapter Twelve

Kit gaped at the vision in a cream silk creation. This was his little waif? With color in her cheeks, a serene smile, and an aura of happiness around her, she glided into the room like a queen.

Forgetting whatever he'd been saying to Daubrey, Kit moved to her side. She smelled amazing too. Her perfume was feminine and mysterious. Taking her hand in his, he raised it to his lips and kissed it. "You look beautiful."

Her endearing blush returned. "You do, too."

"In truth?" He struck a pose. "You think so?"

Her color deepened but she didn't duck her head. Instead, she raised her chin and met his gaze boldly. "Yes. I've never seen such a beautiful man."

"Careful." He grinned. "You might feed my arrogance too much."

A charmingly teasing glitter entered her eyes. "You are also a talented musician. Have I told you that?"

He affected a pout. "No, I don't believe you have. I was feeling rather out of sorts that you hadn't fed my pride yet."

She laughed softly. "Speaking of music, why aren't you playing tonight?"

He tucked her hand into the crook of his arm. "I told Alex I had a vexing family obligation so the second chair is taking my place. Besides, I cannot bear to play that duet with anyone but you. The other principal harpist simply doesn't perform with as much heart as you."

She smiled so dazzlingly that he nearly dropped to his knees and begged her to marry him. He pictured spending his days with her, taking her on long rambles through the grounds around their home. He imagined teaching her to ride, and having picnics in a grassy meadow. Lastly, he conjured up images of a houseful of children playing music and laughing and chasing each other. The thought of marrying Susanna conjured warmth and a sense of completion.

She stood near enough that each motion, each breath sent shivers of awareness through him. Her intriguing scent—flowery, with citrus and something warm, evoked visions of kisses. Yes, he wanted very much to kiss her. He visualized kissing her any time he wanted, and even waking up with her in his arms.

From the foyer, the butler's alarmed voice broke through his thoughts. "You cannot force your way in here. Sir!" Footsteps neared. "Sir!"

"This cannot wait," said a strange male voice.

"My lord!" the butler burst in. "Forgive me, but these men insist on—"

That unfamiliar male voice interrupted. "I have a warrant for the arrest of one Susanna Dyer."

Disbelief chilled Kit's limbs. In the doorway, the harried-looking butler stood next to a grim-faced London constable and the bounder who had made a grab for Susanna in the streets.

"What?" cried Esther.

Susanna sharply drew in her breath. "Oh," she said in tiny voice.

Kit took a protective step in front of her.

Daubrey sprang to action. "How dare you barge into my home?"

As both lawmen stiffened, the constable spoke in apologetic tones. "Sorry gov'na, but she is a thief. I have been instructed to see to it that she returns to face the local magistrate for her crime."

Summoning the imperious expression he'd so often seen in his father and that of his brother, Kit held out his hand and commanded, "Show me your warrant."

The constable handed over a document with an official seal at the bottom. Daubrey peered over his shoulder. With his heart turning to stone, Kit glanced at his brother-in-law.

Daubrey nodded. "It's official."

"Ridiculous. I don't believe it," Esther said.

Alarm shot down Kit's back like a hundred

beestings. He called upon every haughty, autocratic bone in his ancestry and drew himself up. "You cannot take her."

"Sir, I understand that this may be—" the constable began.

"Lord." Kit glared at him.

The constable's brow furrowed in puzzlement. "Er...sir?"

Kit drew himself up and sneered. "Do you two thugs have any idea who we are?"

Both men paled and the constable managed an inarticulate. "Ah..."

The man from the country rallied first. "Don't care. She's a criminal, and you are interfering with justice."

Susanna's breath came in tiny gasps. "I'm not a criminal. I've done nothing wrong."

Kit looked down his nose at the cur. If it came to a fair fight, this man, built like a prize fighter, could probably best Kit. Still, Kit had weapons he would not hesitate to unleash. "I am Lord Christopher, son of the Duke of Charlemonte. You are in the home of my brother-in-law and sister, the Viscount and Lady Daubrey. If you think you can take their guest—and my betrothed—without irrefutable proof, you are sadly mistaken."

Susanna sucked in her breath at his use of the

word "betrothed" but kept silent. He didn't dare look
at her. This wasn't the way he'd planned it, but the
words had come tumbling out of him. The hired thug
swallowed and the constable took a step back.

Fisting his hands, Kit pressed, "I require you to
provide proof—and witnesses—of her so-called crime
before I will consider escorting her to face her accusers
and this magistrate who they clearly duped into
swearing out a warrant for her arrest."

The hired man's face reddened. "Absolutely not.
Lord or no lord, you are not above the law, and
neither is your little tart."

Kit's temper snapped and he punched the
bounder square in the face. "How dare you, sirrah!"

The hired man stumbled backwards and lost his
balance. He sprawled on the floor. In a half-inclined
position, he dabbed at his lip and shot a murderous
glare at Kit. "You...."

The constable stepped in between them. "No
need for all this. We can place her under house arrest
and leave her here in the care of...Lord Daubrey, was
it?"

Daubrey inclined his head.

"I'm sure we can get this matter cleared up," the
constable continued. "Please forgive the intrusion,
milords. Milady."

The London constable grabbed his companion

and half-dragged him out, murmuring something about jurisdiction, magistrates, and how things are done in London.

A stunned silence fell.

"Those brutes," Esther said, her eyes snapping. "How dare they come into our home like that."

Kit turned to Susanna. All the color had drained out of her face.

He put a hand on either shoulder and peered into her eyes. "No magistrate will call for your forcible removal from a viscount's home. As long as you stay within the grounds, they cannot touch you."

Trembling, she fixed a sober look at him. "It wasn't necessary for you to lie for me about being your betrothed."

"It will strengthen our claim of protection on you." He smiled. It had felt so natural to declare her to be his intended bride.

"I can't stay here forever—I won't impose on the Daubrey's longer than I must."

"When they can't prove you've actually done anything wrong, they will be forced to drop the charges." He touched her cheek.

"And you know it's no imposition," huffed Esther.

"I still can't imagine why my aunt wants me back. They were so eager to be rid of me."

Kit kept his hand on her cheek. "I'll make inquiries in the morning. Until then, try not to dwell on it." He yearned to hold her close, to reassure and comfort her. He dropped his hand before he did anything to embarrass Susanna. With her so overset, now would be a terrible time to pull her into his arms and kiss her.

Daubrey poured a drink and returned with a glass of sherry. He offered it to Susanna. "Drink. It will settle your nerves."

Susanna shook her head. "I've never had a strong drink."

"Now might be a good time to start," Daubrey said.

"Thank you, but no," Susanna said firmly.

Esther took it. "I need that." She gulped it down.

Susanna stood looking as if she were all alone in the world. Kit gave in to his desires and gently drew Susanna into his arms.

Softly, he said, "I won't let them have you, I vow it."

She let out a little sigh and rested against him. For a blissful moment, Kit basked in the glory of holding her in his arms. She felt so *right*.

Daubrey chuckled. "Well done, Kit. You certainly put those peasants back in their place."

Esther's face relaxed and she joined in with

Daubrey. Kit smiled in spite of himself. He'd never pulled rank like that—he had never felt the need. When his little Susanna was threatened, it had seemed the easiest weapon. He would do whatever he must to keep her safe.

Susanna stiffened and pulled away. "Wait. You said...are you really Lord Christopher? Son of the Duke of Charlemonte?"

He almost groaned out loud. "Yes. Never fear, I'm his youngest son, so I'm in no danger of becoming a duke." He gave her a self-deprecating smile.

Her eyes wide, she took another step back.

He reached for her. "Please don't hold that against me. I'm still Kit."

She twisted her hands and glanced at Esther. "I don't belong here."

Esther gave her a gently scolding look. "Of course you do. You are the daughter of a gentleman and you are my friend. Our friend." She glanced at Kit. Her smile broadened as if some unholy thought buzzed around in her conniving head. Of course. She probably began planning the wedding the moment he used the word betrothed. He grinned at the thought.

Soon, he would make that official. Of course, he probably ought to formally ask Susanna if she would have him before he bought the wedding ring and obtained a license. Wedding ring. Hmm. He had an idea about that.

A footman, dressed in full livery, announced the arrival of their first guest. In all the uproar over the lawmen, Kit had forgotten all about the dinner party.

He glanced at Susanna. Her face was still pale and her hands continued to tremble. He lowered his voice. "Change your mind about that drink?"

She shook her head. He offered her his arm and stood next to her, sending a clear message to all the guests that she and he had an understanding—it wasn't true, of course, since she hadn't exactly agreed to anything despite his declaration to the constable. Still, having her next to him gave him supreme pleasure and instilled a new, quiet confidence he'd never experienced with another woman. He very much wanted to spend the rest of his life with her. The knowledge created a cocoon of peace around him.

Susanna took several deep breaths, visibly calming with each one. By the time they greeted their first guest, Susanna had rallied so completely that no one would have guessed what had transpired only moments ago. She sailed through introductions with all the poise of a seasoned Londoner—warm, genuine, and mildly reticent which only added to her charm.

A fair number of ladies twittered over Kit, making overt comments about how they hadn't seen him in an age and where *had* he been? By the end of the evening, several of the male guests were so enamored of Susanna that Kit didn't dare leave her side or they'd be panting all over her.

Egad, he had not missed the social whirl. A benefit of maintaining the façade of Kit the violin player was that he'd been spared the silly society games, the false smiles, and most of all, living under his father's thumb. He'd taken a chance agreeing to attend his sister's dinner party. Knowing Susanna must face the dragons of society prompted his acquiescence. How glad he was that he'd attended this evening, for more than one reason.

After dinner, games, idle chit chat, and a brief discussion about the war that Daubrey deftly diverted to less weighty matters, the guests finally took their leave. The house fell into silence. The servants seemed to let out a collective breath.

Kit glanced at Susanna. She eyed him soberly. Then she did the unexpected. She laughed. She laughed—a full belly-laugh of such mirth that he couldn't help but join in, even though he had no idea what had set her off. Esther joined in next, and even Daubrey chuckled.

"Whatever is so funny?" Kit finally managed.

Susanna wiped tears from her eyes and shook her head. "It was so absurd. All this time, I had thought the upper class of society would be so very far above me." She lifted her shoulders. Then she sobered, as if stopping herself, and addressed Tess and Daubrey. "I mean no offense to you or your friends."

Still smiling, Tess waved her hand. "Speak your mind, Susanna, you are amid friends. They are surely talking about us."

Susanna hesitated before forging on, "Conversing with them was no more taxing than conversing with villagers of my acquaintance back home. These members of the *ton* were not any wiser or wittier. I cannot imagine why I was so afraid to meet your friends. They were not terrifying in the least. On the contrary, they were really quite delightful and so very *normal*."

Kit took her hand. "You are absolutely right. So no more talk of whether or not you belong among them—in fact, you far outshone the brightest of them."

"I'm sure I did not, but I thank you for saying so." She smiled. "I can't afford the clothing or jewels they wore..."

"That is all they have over you, and easily remedied. All you need is a husband to pay for the clothing you deserve."

She chuckled. "Yes, well, the evening was notably absent of all offers of that kind."

He lifted his brow and cocked his head. "Was it?"

She looked down. "You didn't mean that. It was

205

just a way of telling the constable you were protecting me."

"I did mean it. I do want to marry you. Will you have me?"

Before this past week, he'd never given much thought to marriage. He'd always assumed he might do it someday but had never known anyone with whom he might consider sharing his life. Then he met Susanna. She brought out the best parts of him, the parts of him that were honorable, gallant, protective, strong. She reminded him of the importance of family. He wanted to be with her. He wanted to make music and laughter and children with her.

She went very still and her eyes grew round.

He took her hand. "This isn't how it's done, but since your father and brother are gone, and your uncle is out of your life, I have no one to ask permission."

"Kit...."

"I know this is sudden. We haven't known each other long." He swallowed. This was probably the wrong way to go about it, but he forged ahead. "You are the one I've been looking for. Please, will you do me the very great honor of becoming my wife?"

Her breathing came fast and she took a step back. "You can't be in earnest."

"I don't care who your father is, and I don't care if you have little to no dowry. Please, marry me?"

She shook her head helplessly. "Kit..."

"I can take care of you, protect you from your relatives and men like that thug your aunt sent after you."

She folded her hands and all the light in her eyes dimmed. "I'm sorry. My answer is no." She curtsied formally, nodded to Esther and Daubrey. "Thank you for a lovely evening. I shall retire now."

As she walked away from him, Kit stood, trying not to fold under the sensation that he'd been kicked in the stomach.

"Oh, Kit." Esther put her hand over her mouth, her eyes bright with tears.

"Good night, Tess. Daubrey." Empty down to his soul, he strode out of the house and into the night, alone.

Chapter Thirteen

Susanna held onto her composure until after Polly helped her out of her gown and stays, blew out the candles, and left. Only then did Susanna curl up and allow her tears to flow. She sobbed like a child. She'd found the man of her dreams, a man she loved beyond all her hopes and expectations, but he only viewed her as an object of charity. He only saw her as a pitiable waif in need of protection. He was gallant enough to go through with his impromptu marriage proposal. Eventually, however, he would realize he had made a terrible mistake. He'd been kind to her but he clearly did not love her. How could he? He deserved someone beautiful and polished, and preferably the daughter of a peer—or at the very least a member of the gentry with a respectable dowry.

How tempting it had been to accept! He offered her safety and all the basic necessities of life. But the thought of marrying someone who did not love her and who might grow to regret his alliance with her, left her cold and empty.

In addition to add to that sad truth, he was the son of a duke. No one of his rank should marry someone as poor and unimportant as she.

She would make all haste to find employment and leave. Though she'd miss her dear friend Esther terribly, remaining here under her roof after rejecting her brother's kind offer would be unconscionable. Worse, Susanna risked seeing Kit time and again, continually reminded of who she desperately wanted, needed, loved, yet could not have.

After meeting with his attorney and giving him a very specific assignment, Kit walked several miles to his parent's London house. He stood on the drive leading to the portico in front of the house. Though he spent most of his childhood in the country when he wasn't at school, a range of memories flitted over him of times he'd spent in this house as well—playing with his brother and cousins, and pretending he didn't want his little sister tagging along, learning to ride, violin lessons, outings to the park and museums and private zoos, and even his first kiss.

Over it all loomed the shadow of his father, always correcting, prodding, disapproving, and generally managing every aspect of Kit's life. And when Kit had learned first-hand the horrors of slavery in their plantations, he'd been unable to enjoy any luxury of home. Once Kit left, without bending to accept even a single farthing of his allowance, he had experienced a measure of freedom and satisfaction that only comes from self-reliance, as well as a sense of pride at his accomplishments that he'd never experienced before. Still, he missed his father. He missed their lively debates, the chess games, the knowledge that if he encountered an obstacle too big to manage, he could turn to his father for help. That help might come with a price, but he'd always been secure that he wasn't expected to face all his challenges alone. Since he left home, he'd been alone. Oh, he had friends, and his music, but they failed to take the place of family. He'd been alone for far too long.

Squaring his shoulders, Kit marched up the drive and into the house.

"Lord Christopher, your mother is in her morning parlor," the butler greeted him.

"Is my father at home?" Kit asked.

"No, my lord, he left early this morning."

Mingled relief and sorrow warred within him. After all the time he'd spent preparing himself for a conversation with his father, he would not have the opportunity to see him today.

Kit strode to his mother's morning room and found her sitting at her writing desk, penning a letter. "Good morning, Mother."

She looked up and dropped her pen. "Why, Christopher, what a delightful surprise." She came to him and took his hands. She looked him carefully in the eyes. "Tell me what has you so blue-deviled this lovely morning."

He sat with her and carefully lined up each finger with the matching finger on the opposite hand. "I met someone."

"The harpist?"

He lifted his head. "You know?"

"Esther told me. She wanted me to know that she approves even though the girl is an orphan and a professional musician."

Good ol' Esther. He almost smiled, but his heart was too heavy. "Her name is Susanna Dyer. She is remarkable, so unspoiled and sweet, but she's not at all a green, missish girl from the country. She's genuine and has this sort of serenity about her. She's remarkably uncomplaining despite how her relatives have clearly misused her."

"So her being a penniless orphan wanted by the law does not deter you?"

"Those charges are false, and I mean to prove it." Too agitated to sit, he got up and paced. "As to her being a penniless orphan—it is of no consequence. I haven't known her for very long, but she's unlike anyone I've ever met." He paused, then said the words in his heart. "I love her."

His mother smiled gently and clasped her hands together. "Does she know?"

He paced faster, turning on his heel each time he reached a wall. "Yes. I asked her to marry me, but she refused me."

"Oh, my..."

A flood of words poured out of him. "I don't know if it's because when she found out who I am she doesn't feel as if she belongs—perhaps she worries you and Father won't approve or society will be unkind to her. Maybe she's angry I didn't tell her who my family connections were from the start, or ...." He swallowed. "Or if she simply doesn't return my regard."

She might have no wish to shackle herself to a man she didn't love. Had he misread her admiring glances? Had he arrogantly assumed she cared for him without truly exploring her feelings?

He'd never doubted his appeal to the fair sex. They'd always admired him. Even those who didn't know his rank and social status clearly found him physically attractive.

What if Susanna did not? Self-doubt, an almost unknown sensation until now, spiraled through him.

"Christopher."

He stopped pacing.

Quietly Mother asked, "Did you tell her you love her?"

"I...." he trailed off. Had he actually told her he loved her? He was pretty sure he had, and that he'd said something about feeling complete when he was with her. Hadn't he?

"Oh, my dear boy." She shook her head. "You need to make that clear. She might think you are offering for her out of a desire to protect her from the law—a chivalrous gesture to be sure, but a young lady wants to know that she is loved."

He sat. He'd probably botched the whole thing. Perhaps the timing had been bad. He'd asked her at the end of the evening—after the constable and the hired brute had threatened to take her away. Kit had acted like a pompous boor in his desire to protect her. She might have thought he felt some sort of misplaced obligation or overblown chivalry.

What to do now? At a loss, he hunched over and rested his elbows on his knees. She'd already been the victim of pushy men who wanted her for all the wrong reasons. Did he dare press his suit again?

"Son." Mother moved to his side and put a hand on his back. "If she's as sweet and big-hearted as Esther says, she will give you another chance."

His fears burst out of him. "What if she simply doesn't want me?"

"Then you have a choice; you can either woo her with all the energies of your heart or you can give her up with the belief that if she doesn't see all your fine qualities—the good and kind and honorable man that you are—she isn't good enough for you."

Give her up? Let her walk out of his life? The idea sent waves of panic over him.

His mother leaned back against the cushions of the sofa. "Your father had to fight for me, you know."

"He did?" He lifted his head.

"I wasn't sure I liked him. He seemed too stern." She chuckled softly. "He didn't give up, and I eventually saw the tender heart he keeps hidden from others. He loves very deeply, but he was raised to keep those emotions buried, to maintain proper decorum. It took me a fair amount of time to see that about him. I'm glad he was persistent." She smiled with a faraway look in her eyes.

"I can be persistent."

Mother put her arm around him and squeezed his shoulders. He leaned against her. Hunching over, he rested his head on her shoulder. Finally, he gave in to his instincts; he closed his eyes and allowed his mother's love to fill him with healing confidence.

He would not let Susanna go without doing everything in his power to win her over. "Thank you, Mother."

She kissed his brow and pressed her forehead against his. "Go fight for your lady."

"I will." He stood.

As he crossed the main hall to the exit, the door opened and admitted his father. Kit halted. His father, the Duke of Charlemonte, handed his hat and gloves to the butler. He glanced at Kit. He froze. Wearing a Cambridge blue coat and buff knee breeches, his hessian boots shining like glass, the duke stood as if a soldier at attention. He was stiff, proper, and meticulous as always. His impassive stare dried Kit's mouth.

Kit swallowed. "Good morning." He almost added *Your Grace* but clamped his mouth shut.

The duke's expression never changed but he inclined his head as if greeting an associate. "Lord Christopher." Always formal. Stiff. Disapproving.

"I..." Kit took a breath.

His father waited.

Kit swallowed.

Something in the duke's expression softened. He gestured. "Would you care to join me in my study?"

Kit nodded. As he waited for the duke to reach his side, Kit studied his father. In the two years since Kit had seen him last, his father had aged. He still walked with confidence and power, yet more silver streaked his dark hair, more wrinkles lined his eyes and mouth.

"Are you...well?" Kit asked.

"I am quite well, thank you. And you?"

"Yes. Thank you."

The small talk fizzled out. They reached the study

and entered. Nothing had changed. Heavy dark furniture and scarlet wallpaper still adorned the study. His ducal desk presided over the room as it always had. Their chess table sat near the window where it always had, the silver pieces lined up and ready for the next battle. It was like coming home.

The duke picked up a crystal decanter. "Care for a sherry or brandy?"

"No, thank you."

His father poured himself a glass. "If you are here to receive my blessing on your wedding to this little musician with whom you and Esther seem so infatuated, you are of age. I cannot naysay you. Are you here to transfer your unused allowance into your own account?"

"No, I actually came to see you. It's been too long."

He paused. Then, "I see."

They stood awkwardly. His father drank. Kit stared at the darkened hearth.

Kit's gaze fell on the chessboard, and he gestured. "Do you still play?"

"Not since you left."

Kit chewed on that information.

Father nodded toward the chessboard. "Care to play now?"

"I believe we are overdue."

They played chess. As they matched move for move, the years fell away. A comforting sense of home came over him. At first, their conversation stuttered, lighting on minor subjects such as the weather, the political arena, the news. They played through luncheon and tea, enjoying those repasts as they played and talked. Eventually, they discussed estate matters. Later, Kit told his father about his position as concertmaster with a respectable orchestra, and how much he enjoyed playing with other musicians. Kit eventually told him about Susanna—how they met, how much he enjoyed creating music with her. He even admitted the boxing his father insisted that he do in his youth had come in handy when defending Susanna from the lawman. He skirted around his feelings for her, and left out his clumsy proposal.

His father, stoic as always, finally unbent enough to let his expression soften and his mouth actually curved into something resembling a smile. "You have your head on straight, son. And a good heart. I trust your judgment."

Kit blinked and cleared his throat to hide just how much those words meant to him. "Thank you." He focused on the game and moved a piece.

By dinnertime, his father had beaten him, but only just. They stood and shook hands.

"Don't stay away so long next time, son." His father looked away and cleared his throat.

"I won't." Kit took a few steps away, then turned back. "It was good to see you, Father."

He received a silent nod in reply.

Astonishing. His ever-controlling father had not tried to correct or control him in any way. He mostly listened, as if Kit were an equal.

At the door, his father's voice stopped him. "Bring her here to meet us. I promise not to eat her."

"I will, if she'll have me. I haven't won her over yet."

"War and love are not for the fainthearted. Have courage." He shook his fist as if rallying the troops.

Kit smiled. He'd come expecting a confrontation but had only received encouragement. Had his father changed, or had Kit? Perhaps a little of both. "Good day, sir."

"Good day, son."

As Kit headed for the door, his father called out, "You might be interested to know that I closed the plantations and freed the slaves. All of them."

Kit gaped. Had he heard correctly?

"It will take years to recover from the loss," the duke continued, "unless the canal venture pays off better than I hope it will."

Too weak to stand under the magnitude of what his father said, Kit sat. "Are we bankrupt?"

"No, of course not. We'll have a few lean years

but I've invested in other ventures that do not involve the slave trade, and I've let out the houses in Bath and Kent as well as the hunting lodge. Your mother will never know—she hadn't visited any of those places in years. And no, this won't affect her pin money or allowance—that's all safely in a trust fund."

Kit continued to grapple with the news. "What did Dunlap think of this?" As the heir, his brother stood to lose a great deal on this decision.

"He conceded to my wishes."

Kit spread his hands. "I don't know what to say."

"It was worth it to gain the respect of my son." His father quirked the closest thing to a smile Kit had ever seen. It was fleeting, but it was there. He resumed his usual stoic demeanor and sat. "I have some correspondence I need to attend to."

Kit stood. "Thank you, Father. For everything."

He gave his father a low, formal bow. Still reeling over his father's revelation—his sacrifice—Kit walked home. He'd had no idea his good opinion mattered that much to the duke.

How lean, exactly, would the next few years be for his family? His father had promised that his mother would never feel the tightening of their purse strings. Still, his conscience pricked him that his father and brother would feel the strain. It had to be worth it, though, if it meant their family would no longer

219

engage in slavery. Perhaps someday, such a vile practice would be abolished everywhere.

Kit returned home significantly lighter of heart, and changed for the upcoming evening performance.

At the theatre, he continued looking for Susanna, even knowing she would not be there. He felt remarkably unsupported without her there and when his duet with the principal harpist came, it felt forced and empty. The harpist attacked the music as if he were trying to beat it into a shape it was never meant to take. At the end, Kit glanced back. The musician muttered and tugged on his hair, then he stroked the harp with both hands and nuzzled it as if they were lovers rather than musician and instrument. Kit frowned. He really suspected the man was, as a violin teacher used to say, "a note short of a full scale." Was he truly mad or just egregiously eccentric?

At the end of the concert, Alex raised his brows. "You didn't have your heart in it tonight, Kit."

Kit shook his head. "Any chance we could offer Susanna the job of secondary harpist, or even give her the duet exclusively? She is a better harpist, and you know it."

Nearby, laughter rang out over the murmur of voices.

"I'll discuss it with the manager and see what we can do," Alex promised.

"Thank you."

One of the female musicians paused next to him. "Are you still courting Susanna, Kit?"

Orchestra gossip must have chewed on his obvious interest in the temporary harpist. He answered in what he hoped would be the truth as soon as he convinced Susanna to give him another chance. "I am. Why do you ask?"

"When I heard she was no longer needed, I was concerned for her. She is so sweet but so very green." She smiled. "If you are courting her then I'm sure you must be seeing to it that she is well."

"She is very well, indeed." He tried to smile but his heavy heart tugged too hard at the memory of her refusal.

"Oh, I'm so happy to hear it." The cellist smiled. "I miss her. She played so well—so much better than our regular harpist. Everyone is saying so."

"She certainly does." The wistfulness in his voice taunted his own ears.

He looked forward to a lifetime of hearing her music. If he managed to convince her to have him, he would give her a harp for a wedding gift, and she could play all she wanted. He really ought to procure more harp-violin duets so they could play together. An almost feverish desire to see Susanna again seized him. Forgoing his usual stop at the Silver Duck, he fairly trotted to Esther's house.

Inside the Daubrey's house, the strains of a harp guided him to the drawing room. He found Esther snuggled up against Daubrey on an Ottomane couch, their fingers intertwined, their heads close together. Envy arose at the sight. He ached to share such moments with Susanna. She sat at the Louis XVI harp, playing so mournfully that his eyes burned in response.

Did she play with such sorrow because she feared her fate? If only her sadness stemmed from missing him. Did he dare hope she regretted her hasty answer to his proposal?

Careful not to make a sound, he sank into the nearest chair and watched her hands move gracefully over the strings like the arms of a ballerina, coaxing from the harp such poignantly beautiful tones that he feared he'd break down and weep on the spot.

The final notes died away. Kit swallowed against the lump in his throat.

Esther sniffled. "That was heartbreaking."

"Yes, it was," Kit said softly.

"Kit, I didn't see you come in." Susanna stood and clasped her hands together. She fidgeted and glanced at Esther and Daubrey. "How was the performance tonight?"

"Not nearly as moving as when you play with me."

Her mouth curved into a sad smile. "I shall miss that." She looked away.

He stood and took a few steps closer. "I asked Alex to speak to the manager about making you the secondary harpist, and even suggested that he give you the duet to play every night."

She looked down. "That was kind of you."

He moved to her side. "I didn't do it out of kindness. I did it because you play it better than the other harpist does. He's technically good, but you play with such emotion that it creates magic."

Her smile widened but she refused to look at him. He took her hand and tugged gently. "Will you walk with me?"

She wrapped her fingers around his hand. A promising response. He led her outside to the terrace and took her to a bench next to the railing within sight of their chaperones. Esther and Daubrey pointedly kept their attention on each other and began conversing perhaps more loudly than necessary. Kit sent his intuitive sister a silent thank you. Moonlight cast a soft halo around Susanna. The sharp planes of her cheekbones had softened, probably due to his sister feeding her practically every hour, and she no longer had the wary, half-starved look of the little waif who'd lingered at the stage door desperate for an audition. Even then, he'd sensed something about her, an inner drive, a quiet strength. Over the last few days, a new confidence had settled over her like a favorite shawl.

"I owe you an apology," he began.

She fixed her eyes on him, too shadowed in the moonlight for him to see them clearly or to judge her mood. "For what are you apologizing?"

"I didn't deliberately deceive you about who I am, but I didn't tell you the whole truth, either. I left home, determined to reject everything of my father's and to be my own man. I have been living the life of a musician for so long that it comes naturally to me now." He drew a breath. "For more than two years, I had stopped thinking of myself as anyone other than merely Kit Anson, a violinist."

Quietly and without looking at him, she said, "You don't have to explain anything to me."

"Susanna, I give you my word I was not trying to withhold anything from you."

She cast a quick glance at him and lifted her shoulder in a shrug. "'Tis of no consequence."

She remained so distant, almost untouchable. He ached to restore that comfortable connection they once shared. She arose and took several steps away, out of the light from the drawing room.

With a rustle of foliage, a dark shape leaped out at her. Moonlight flashed silver off a knife. The figure raised his arm up, and plunged the blade downward at Susanna. She let out a cry and collapsed.

224

Chapter Fourteen

Pain exploded in Susanna's chest and her breath rushed out of her. A weak scream burst out. She fell to the ground under the force of the blow. The shadowy figure raised his arm to deliver another blow.

Kit leaped at the attacker. Their bodies collided and thudded on the terrace floor. The sickening crunch of a fist hitting flesh, and then a male grunt reached her ears. A metallic clang rang out and a silvery blade slid across the marble terrace. Soon, noises combined too quickly for Susanna to follow.

With each breath, her chest throbbed. Almost afraid at what she'd find, she looked down at her chest. Nothing. No stains. She sat up. Despite her motion, the pain faded. She got to her feet and picked up the blade so the assailant couldn't use it on Kit.

Still scrabbling, Kit fell back and let out a curse.

"Susanna?" Esther's voice reached her ears.

Esther and Daubrey stepped out. "Are you—?" she gasped as her gaze traveled downward to the dagger in Susanna's hand.

The attacker ran off into the night.

Kit leaped to his feet and started after him but paused and looked back at her. "Susanna?"

She let out a weak, stunned huff of laughter. "I'm unharmed."

"You're sure?"

She tapped her chest. "Never better."

He raced off. She bit her lip. Oh dear, he'd just raced off in pursuit of a dangerous man. At least, the attacker was no longer armed...unless he had another weapon concealed. Had Kit plunged into a trap where others lay in wait for him?

"Go help Kit!" Susanna pointed in the direction both men had taken.

Without a word, Daubrey dashed after them.

Esther ran to her. "Are you hurt?"

"No."

She pressed her fingers on her chest where the blade had struck. It hurt, but dully, more like a bruise rather than the wound a blade should have caused. Gently, she tapped her chest, encountering the center boning that ran right down between her breasts. She leaned over and peered at her gown, probing. The silk fabric gaped open where it had been sliced apart, and the heavy muslin fabric of her stays also opened to reveal the boning sewn in.

Susanna met Esther's wide eyes. "Someone tried to stab me." She lifted the knife and examined it. A long, narrow dagger gleamed in the moonlight.

"Good heavens! Your stays saved you." Esther's

breathing rasped. "Who would want to hurt you? Your aunt?"

Susanna shook her head. "The man my aunt sent surely wants me alive if he means to collect on his payment."

Esther put an arm around Susanna. They stood together, grim and silent.

Susanna peered into the darkness and listened for Kit and Daubrey. "Do you think they are safe?"

"I'm sure they are. They are both capable men."

"But the man who attacked me is—"

"Surely no match for them alone, much less them together."

Arm-in-arm, they peered into the dark foliage, eyes and ears straining for any signs of the gentlemen. If Kit hurt his hands badly enough, he would be unable to play the violin. That would be tragic. She silently prayed for his safety.

Moments later, footsteps and voices alerted them. Two figures came tearing around a bend in the garden path. Susanna's heart thumped as she strained for the sight of Kit. Finally, he appeared. She let out an agonized breath. He was safe!

Kit let out a sound like a wounded animal and raced to her, touching her face, looking her over. "I thought I'd lost you," he said roughly. He pulled her to him. "I don't know what I would have done if something had happened to you." His voice revealed true concern. For her.

Susanna wrapped her arms around him and sagged against him. His breath came in hard gasps, and his heart raced against her cheek. He held her close and rested his cheek on top of her head. How lovely to have someone worry over her. How sublime to bask in the euphoria of his arms around her. She let out a sigh, and her shaking subsided. In his arms, she was safe and...dare she say it? Loved? Did he truly love her as he said? He certainly seemed alarmed beyond simple kindness or the desire to help a penniless musician.

"When I saw that blade..." he pulled away. "How is it possible he didn't harm you?" His gaze moved downward.

Susanna blushed as he studied the center of her chest, not the leer of a brute, but the inspection of a concerned friend. Still, to have a man look at her there...

In wonder, he said, "Your gown is cut but you aren't injured. How...?"

Esther replied. "Somehow, the center boning of her stays stopped the blade."

Susanna's blush heated. She'd never imagined discussing ladies' undergarments with a male. To reassure Kit, she said, "I may be a bit bruised, but I'm not injured."

"Come inside," Daubrey urged as he glanced around. "It may not be safe."

Kit pulled away and said grimly, "The assailant got away."

He released her enough to turn them both toward the open French doors. With one arm around her shoulders, he guided her inside. Once they reached the middle of the drawing room, he stopped and embraced her again. She rested against him and let out a sigh, releasing the rest of her fright. Nothing in her life had prepared her for the sweet sensation of Kit holding her.

"Did you get a look at him?" Daubrey asked Kit.

Kit's expression tightened. "I didn't see his face. I lost him in the street before I could identify him..." His voice hardened. "...or bring him back to answer for what he did."

"Can you describe anything about him?" Looking in a mirror, Daubrey smoothed back his mussed hair and straightened his disheveled cravat.

Without releasing Susanna, Kit said, "Slender build, similar to me, and a few inches shorter, I think."

Daubrey sat nearby. "Not big enough to have been the country thug, then. Do you have any idea who he was, Miss Dyer?"

Susanna shook her head. "He was unfamiliar to

me. I don't know anyone in London, certainly not well enough to have made an enemy." A few ladies at the previous night's party who were vying for Kit's attention had glared at her, but none of them looked capable of exerting themselves enough to plot her demise.

Kit let go of her and paced away but came back and took her hand as if he needed to touch her.

"Perhaps we're looking at this wrong," Daubrey said. "What if someone went after her to strike at you?"

Kit paused, his eyes darting back and forth as if recalling his past. "If anyone hates me that much, I am unaware of it."

"We should report this to the night watch and to the magistrate," Daubrey said. "They need to know someone is after her."

Esther scoffed. "The constable was no help the other night when he and that brute showed up demanding to take her away."

While Daubrey and Esther launched into a debate, Kit turned to Susanna and looked her over carefully. She took his hands and examined them, turning them over. Faint bruises married his knuckles.

"Did you hurt your hands?" she asked.

He flexed his fingers. "Nothing that will prevent me from performing."

She raised his bruised hands to her lips and kissed them. "I'm sorry you were hurt."

He huffed a weak laugh. "Sweet Susanna, have no concern for me. I'm still amazed you weren't wounded." He cradled her cheek with one hand and looked intently into her eyes. "I realize my manner of proposing left something to be desired." He drew a breath. "I love you. "

Susanna's breath rushed out of her.

"When I asked you to marry me, I wasn't trying to rescue you. I love you. I want you in my life. When you are near me, I am strong and confident. Complete. You make me feel as though I have a place in the world and something important to offer."

Her lower lip quivered. "Truly?"

He cupped her cheek. "You are all that is kind and good. I am better just for knowing you. I know we haven't known each other very long, and I very much wish to court you properly to give you time to determine your feelings for me. Just know that I love you so very much—enough for a lifetime. For many lifetimes."

The realization that he truly cared for her beyond simple chivalric duty warmed her all over. She finally let go of her reservations and a flood of love for him came rushing out like waters of a broken dam. Healing warmth and wholeness filled her up until she thought she'd burst from joy.

A tear trickled down her cheek. "Oh, Kit."

Earnest, almost desperate, he tugged on her hands and looked her directly in the eyes. "I meant what I said. I love you. I want you for my wife. I'm willing to wait until you want that, too—until you are sure. Please, will you at least allow me to court you?"

"You...wish to court me?"

A playful twinkle entered his eye. "Unless you're willing to run off to Gretna Green right now and marry me as soon as we can find a blacksmith and an anvil."

She laughed softly at his audacity. How could she refuse? His parents might dislike her for an upstart mushroom, but she would bear any criticism if it meant having Kit in her life.

Smiling so hard that her cheeks stretched, she smiled and nodded. "Of course you may court me."

He kissed her. The warmth and softness of his lips caught her off guard, as did the furious hot tingles spiraling out in all directions. A question lingered in his kiss. She tried to reply in her inexperienced way. He pulled away for only a heartbeat before kissing her again, this time with more intensity, more fervor. His arms wrapped around her and he held her close. This second kiss held a promise. A lifetime of passion surely awaited them. She opened up herself to his love, binding her heart more tightly to his. All her dreams and Sweet Memories had not prepared her for the exhilarating joy that rippled over her like rings in a pond, spreading outward until they filled her. If being married gave her more moments like this, she welcomed it. Yes, he could court her. But she wouldn't ask him to do it for very long. She was already sure.

Her heart sang.

Chapter Fifteen

In his bachelor's rooms the morning after Susanna agreed to let him court her, Kit stared at the letter in his hands, convinced he'd read it wrong. He read it yet a third time.

"Egads, this is a strange development," he muttered.

As the truth of his attorney's letter sank in, he let out a shout, leaped up, and rang for his valet. Calling upon anyone so early in the morning pushed the limits of courtesy, even a sister—especially considering how late they'd gone to bed. Kit had been filled with energy from that unforgettable kiss, and the few more that followed until Esther threw him out. He grinned at the thought.

Finally shaved and dressed, Kit practically ran all the way to Daubrey's house. He burst in and demanded to see his sister at once.

Esther appeared at the railing of the second floor, putting on a wrapper and glaring at him. "You had better have a good explanation for this," she grumbled.

"I need to see Susanna and you...and Daubrey if he's up."

"No one is up," she grumbled. "It's the crack of dawn, you idiot. We only made you leave out a few hours ago."

Kit waved the paper. "This can't wait. I just received news that can clear Susanna's name."

Esther let out a groan, but moments later found Kit in an outer sitting room with Daubrey, Esther, and Susanna. His sweet little harpist looked adorable with her hair hanging around her shoulders and her eyes sleepy.

He wanted to drag her into his arms and kiss her over and over, but settled for kissing her hand. "You are of much greater consequence than you let on, and probably more than you know."

Her brow wrinkled, and she shook her head. "I don't know what you mean."

"My attorney made some inquiries. Your father was Geoffrey Dyer?"

Susanna nodded. "That's right."

"He was the fourth son of William Dyer, who is the second son of the Earl of Clifton. Is that right?"

"Right, again." Her bewilderment was so endearing that he had to stand or he'd surely kiss her right then. "My great-grandfather was the Earl of Clifton."

"Clifton," Daubrey muttered. "Upon my word,"

"On your mother's side, you are also a distant

235

cousin of both the Duke of Suttenberg and the Earl of Tarrington."

Esther let out a gasp. "She's not only a granddaughter of the Earl of Clifton, but she's related to Suttenberg *and* Tarrington?"

Daubrey laughed softly and shook his head in amusement...or perhaps disbelief.

Susanna went completely still. She blinked, shook her head, and blinked again. "I've read enough of my uncle's cast off newspapers that I've heard of these auspicious individuals, but..." Looking thoroughly befuddled, she asked, "Am I really related to them?"

"You didn't know?" Kit asked.

She spread her hands. "I was thirteen when my parents died, and they weren't ones for bragging about their connections. My aunt didn't exactly extol the virtues of my family. She thought hers vastly superior. Honestly, it didn't occur to me to do any research into my heritage. I never cracked open the pages of Debrett's Peerage."

Kit smiled. No, he gloated. "There's more. Your dowry is significant. It is all of forty thousand pounds."

A stunned silence blanketed the room.

"Good heavens," Esther breathed.

Susanna let out a half chuckle. "No, surely not.

My aunt said...." Her voice trailed off. "She lied to me?"

Kit handed her the letter from the attorney as well as a copy of the legal documents. "Read it for yourself."

He waited while she read, her brows furrowing one moment, raising the next.

She shook her head and then met his gaze. "I should have known. She lied to me." Her brow creased. Then she straightened and a hard look came into her eyes. "She lied about everything. *Everything.*"

Kit sat next to her. "It's possible she wanted you to wed Algernon because he agreed to give her part of your dowry."

Her eyes took on a distant stare as she no doubt relived atrocities of her youth. Pain and anger passed over her in alternating strikes, and she winced under each blow. His hand curled into a fist. He didn't know whether to confront the lying blackguards and demand they apologize, or simply cut them from Susanna's life.

Susanna pressed a hand to her head. "That explains a great deal."

Esther smiled. "Oh, Susanna, don't you see? There's no reason for you to think you oughtn't marry Kit."

Susanna turned wide eyes to Kit. "No, there doesn't appear to be...."

He swallowed. Her kisses last night had seemed so promising. Did she harbor doubts now in the light of day?

Searching her face, he took her hand. "You haven't changed your mind, have you? You will still allow me to court you, won't you?"

She met his gaze unflinchingly. For a long moment she said nothing. Kit's heart pounded so hard he feared he'd expire on the spot. Then her mouth curved.

She put a hand on his cheek. "No, Kit, I haven't changed my mind. No need for a courtship. I already know I love you."

He almost forgot to breathe.

The light in her eyes spilled out and filled him. She smiled. "I will marry you, but let's not elope. I want to have a church wedding, and I want your family present."

Joy leaped up and filled every crevice of his heart. He let out a breath that ended with a weak laugh. "Anything, my love." He wrapped her in his arms. "Oh, my sweet Susanna, I love you. I vow I will do all I can to make you happy."

Joyful tears filled her eyes. "My dearest Kit, you already have."

That night, Kit arrived at the theatre early with his thoughts filled with Susanna. His future with her seemed bright with promise and joy. The opera had three more days scheduled to run before closing night, and only Kit's commitment brought him there this evening. As soon as the opera closed, Kit would end his career as a violinist and spend his evenings with the love of his life. Once his attorney finished clearing Susanna of the false charges laid against her by her greedy family, Kit and Susanna would wed and begin their life together.

As he tuned and warmed up, other members of the orchestra came in, their voices and instruments creating a familiar raucous.

The principal harpist came in, and something about his movements caught Kit's attention. The harpist limped and seemed to move stiffly. Kit watched him. Did he have a blackened eye?

Arpeggios on the harp rang out, a much harsher tone than those Susanna's softer touch created as again the opera harpist attacked the instrument as if he meant to bend it to his will. How different from the gentle touch Susanna used to coax beauty from the harp.

The harpist glanced at him and quickly looked away. His hair stuck out all over as if he'd been tugging on it. Was there a patch missing over his ear? Kit took a closer look at the musician, noting his swollen, purple eye. There had been no such visible injuries on the man during the prior evening's performance. What had happened to him since then?

He sauntered over to the harpist. "Meet with another accident?"

The harpist gave a start. "Oh, er, no. I just....fell." He glanced at Kit with annoyance and—was that malice?—but covered it up by tuning the harp.

As the harpist tuned, his hands caught Kit's attention. They appeared reddened, as if they'd recently been used to punch something. Or someone. If Kit were to hazard a guess, the musician looked as if he'd been in a fight.

The memory of the fight with Susanna's attacker sprang into his mind. During the scuffle, Kit had punched the blackguard in the eye. He could not be certain which one, however. Surely the harpist's blackened eye was a coincidence. The harpist would have no reason to attack Susanna. They'd never even met.

"No damage to your hands, I hope?" Kit said conversationally.

"I can play just fine—better than that upstart little tramp you've been seen all over town with."

Kit gaped at the venom coming from the man's mouth. He took a step forward "She is a lady, and I won't have you besmirching her reputation."

"I heard what you said to the conductor about

her being better than I am. Half the orchestra heard it. No little tramp from the country plays as well as I. This is *my* position. My harp."

Cold chills raced down Kit's back. "It was you—in the garden. You stabbed her!"

The harpist lowered his gaze and said sullenly. "I don't know what you're talking about. But if she got stabbed, then she had it coming." A strange light of...madness?...entered his eyes.

Kit relived their fight, recalling every punch. He had wrested the knife out of the attacker's hand, hit the man in the eye, and punched him in the stomach. The opponent had fallen in his flight to get away from Kit but had leaped up and ran with a limp through the garden gate out into the street. Kit had lost him in the darkness.

The harpist had a blackened eye and a limp. His ribs probably pained him.

Kit dredged up a smile and said, "Well then, you probably aren't sore here." He pressed on the harpist's ribs on the left side.

The harpist grunted, his face twisted in pain. "Hands off me, swine."

"It was you." Kit fisted his hands.

A crowd formed around them.

Kit took another step toward the harpist. "After you stabbed Susanna, I punched you in the eye and

241

the stomach, and you twisted your ankle running from me."

"No one touches my lady." He stroked the harp and crooned to it.

Kit folded his arms when he wanted to put a fist through his face. "You might be interested to know that you failed to harm Miss Dyer; she is perfectly well."

The harpist's eyes widened and then grew dark. "The little tart. She won't be so lucky next time."

Kit's vision turned red. He punched the blackguard. Probably too many times. Eventually someone dragged Kit off the sobbing harpist, who continued to gesture at his harp, calling it his lady. The authorities took the mad harpist into custody where he would be of no further threat.

Chapter Sixteen

Just outside the Daubrey's drawing room, Susanna halted to gather her skittering courage. Seeing her relatives would take more courage than she'd ever possessed—running away and facing an uncertain future had been less terrifying than confronting those from whom she'd run. Kit had seen to it their false charges were dropped, but Susanna needed to face them one more time, if nothing else than for the satisfaction of standing up to them. Witnessing them receive a humbling set down wouldn't hurt, either.

She entered. All her old fears returned the moment Aunt Uriana came into view. Her aunt surveyed the room with mingled envy and disdain. Sitting next to her, Uncle yawned and stared off into space, no more interested in these proceedings than he had been in his niece beyond her ability to play the harp for his enjoyment. It was a wonder he had bestirred himself enough to make the journey. Next to Aunt Uriana sat Cousin Percy and Algernon. Percy's eyes were alight with interest in his surroundings, but Algernon picked at his fingernail, his mouth hanging open in that same vacant expression that she'd come to associate with him unless he was striking a servant or kicking a dog.

Kit sat with all the regal confidence of a king, staring them down as if they were snails in a flower bed. In a nearby leather armchair lounged Daubrey, wearing the bored indifference of a lord. Next to him sat Esther who glared as if she were about to scratch out someone's eyes.

Seeing her new friends, and especially the man she loved, restored her confidence. She glanced again at the assembly. Her relatives were not all-powerful beings in control of every aspect of her life; they were only thwarted mortals whose selfishness could no longer hurt her.

Kit stood. "Ah, Susanna, my love. How good of you to join us." He crossed the drawing room and took her hand. As he raised it to his lips, he said under his breath. "Are you sure you wish for this meeting? You can still leave now."

She nodded. "I need to do this."

A gentle smile curved his mouth and approval glittered in his eyes. He tucked her arm around his, and led her back to the group where he seated her next to him on a large, upholstered Ottomane couch, leaving their guests to sit on the less comfortable settee all crowded together.

Aunt Uriana looked her over with narrowed eyes.

Susanna cast a glance over them and said evenly, "Good day." Instead of curtsying, she only gave them the briefest incline of her head.

Uncle's expression sharpened, and he looked at her as if he'd never seen her. Percy's eyes traveled over her, widening in appreciation and mild surprise. Algernon only gave her the briefest of glances before he starting chewing on a cuticle and propping up his gouty foot on the low table in front of the settee. Aunt Uriana, however, shot her a stare that might have frozen her solid in seconds, but Susanna straightened and lifted her chin, deflecting her aunt's former power over her.

Daubrey spoke. "Now that we are all together, we can talk this through like civilized adults."

Aunt Uriana let out a humph. "There's little to say, my lord. She ran away from home. She must return at once."

Susanna shook her head. "No aunt. I will not return. Not ever."

Aunt Uriana blustered. "Why, you..."

Kit's thumb caressed Susanna's hand. "Since she is over the age of eighteen, you are no longer her legal guardians. She may live anywhere she pleases and marry whomever she wishes."

Aunt Uriana continued to bluster. "She is supposed to marry my nephew, Algernon. The banns have already been read."

Susanna watched her aunt with mingled disgust and pity. Why had she ever allowed this woman to dominate her? "That is of little consequence. I am engaged to be married to—" she caught herself before she called him Kit—"Lord Christopher, and he is the only one I will accept as my husband."

The blustering turned to true, red-faced anger. "You must marry Algernon or it will scandalize him and label *you*..." she glared, "...as a jilt."

Outrage rose up inside of Susanna. "I never wanted to marry Algernon, and you know it. I only pretended to agree so you wouldn't lock me in my bedchamber and starve me into submission."

With a guilty glance at Kit and the Daubreys, Aunt Uriana said, "Oh, good heavens, what rubbish."

Kit used the same authoritative voice he'd used with the constable. "Susanna may live anywhere she chooses. And that is final. As to her being labeled a jilt, no one will dare speak out against the daughter-in-law of a duke. This..." he glanced at Algernon... "Algernon, was it? Will have to find himself another bride, if anyone will have him."

Algernon frowned and screwed up his face. "But, I—"

Kit cut him off. "Now, let's move on to the next item of consideration. Your charges against her. You hired someone to go after her, claiming that she stole something."

Uncle raised his brows as if this claim were news to him.

"Yes. She stole a piece of jewelry." Aunt Uriana pursed her lips and fidgeted with her sleeve.

Kit's expression was patently disbelieving. "Really?" he drawled. "And you have proof of this?"

Aunt Uriana glowered. "Of course. It went missing the night she left."

Quietly, but with firmness, Susanna demanded, "What jewelry, Aunt?"

Aunt Uriana paused. "A diamond necklace."

"I don't recall ever seeing you wear a diamond necklace." Susanna tilted her head and allowed her disbelief to show.

Her aunt's eyes shifted back and forth as if she were thinking up a new lie. "Well, of course you wouldn't since you were never present during formal dinner parties." She glanced at Kit and Daubrey. "She wasn't 'out,' you see."

"Nineteen and not yet out?" Esther mused. "That is beyond the pale."

Lord Daubrey nodded. "Deuced odd."

Aunt Uriana shifted.

Uncle finally spoke. "I don't remember this diamond necklace."

Aunt Uriana made an impatient sound. "You never notice things like that."

247

Putting steel in her voice, Susanna said, "I've never seen a necklace like that on you or anywhere in the house, and I certainly didn't steal it—nor anything else."

"It is your word against hers." Kit stood, his posture commanding. "Here is what you are going to do. You will drop the charges against Susanna, and you will leave without making any further contact with her, even indirectly. Otherwise, I will make it known that you starved and neglected her, and that you tried to force her to marry your nephew so you could access her dowry."

Four pairs of gaping mouths met her eyes.

Percy recovered first. He stood and offered Susanna a condescending smile. "Cousin, I apologize for all of this difficulty and hope you know I have always held you in high regard."

"Oh, have you?" Susanna asked sweetly. "I seem to regard your proposition was not what an honorable man normally makes to a lady whom he holds in high regard."

Percy cleared his throat and glanced nervously around. "On the contrary, I was trying to save you from a worse fate. If I weren't already married...."

A huff of disbelief came out of Susanna's mouth. "A worse fate than being ruined? I cannot think of it."

"Nor can I." Esther eyed them as if they were all insects she'd decided to squash.

Aunt Uriana fixed a cold stare on her son. "You idiot. She cannot be your mistress—no one gets her dowry if she doesn't marry."

Percy held out a hand. "I didn't know she had a dowry or that you had hoped to gain access to it."

Susanna cut in. "Goodbye, Cousin." She turned to her uncle. "Uncle." She drew a breath, sifting through all she wanted to say. She finally ended with, "Thank you for allowing me to continue to play the harp. Without my abilities as a harpist, I would never have come to London and met Lord Christopher. Aunt Uriana ...." She searched for something gracious to say but came up with nothing. "I trust our paths shall never again cross. Algernon, if you treat parishioners the same way you treat kittens and puppies, I recommend you reconsider the church. I believe it would suit you ill."

Algernon glanced up at her, and let out a strange chortle as if reliving some act of cruelty he'd committed.

Susanna turned dismissively away.

Daubrey straightened. "I believe our interview is over. We expect the charges to be dropped by the end of the day or the morning papers will be filled with all the ugly truths about each of you. Good day." He called for the servants to see their guests out.

A chorus of indignant sounds fell on seemingly

deaf ears. Susanna maintained a serene air until after her aunt, uncle, and cousins left.

Kit took her into his arms. "Well done, love. I am surprised you aren't even a bit overset."

As Daubrey and Esther slipped out, Susanna rested against him. "They aren't worth the effort. I forgive them so that I shall never think of them again." She lifted her eyes and gazed into his. "From now on, I will only think of you and our life together."

"And perhaps some music."

"Oh, I have no doubt that we will make much beautiful music. I'm sure Esther and Daubrey will allow us to play their harp."

"Or perhaps you'll play your own harp."

She paused, searching his eyes.

"As part of my inheritance, I own a small estate at the south eastern coast. It has a music room...with a harp."

She let out a delighted gasp. "Oh Kit!"

"And." He grinned, obviously pleased with himself. "I have something for you." Looking equal parts smug and handsome, Kit reached into his pocket and opened his hand. "I was waiting for the right time to give this to you."

In his hand lay a small gold and sapphire ring. Could it be? "That looks like my mother's wedding ring." She shook her head. "I sold that to get to London."

"Yes, and I found the pawn where you sold it and I bought it back for you. Mrs. Griffin sends her regards."

Her eyes stung, and the gold and blue dissolved into a watercolor painted by her tears. "Oh, Kit." She picked up the ring and slid it on her finger. "Thank you."

"Is there anything else I can do for you?"

An impish side of her raised its head. "Well, since you're in such a generous mood, there is a parlor maid in my aunt's house named Martha. I would very much like to offer her a job in our home, if that's agreeable to you."

He lifted a brow. "Really? A parlor maid?"

"She was instrumental in helping me reach London," Susanna explained.

A soft light entered Kit eyes. "Then I owe her a debt of gratitude as well. Consider it done."

"Thank you." She kissed him, their lips and hearts meeting in joy and hope and light, promising a future of many more such moments.

"I love you, Susanna, and I want you with me always."

She sighed. "I have been unwanted and unloved for a very long time. It almost seems an unattainable dream to know that you do."

"Not a dream—truth."

She wrapped her arms around his waist. "And I love you so very much, I cannot even express it."

"Try."

She did. She poured out her love through her kiss.

When she'd left home in search of freedom in London, she'd had so little hope of finding anything beyond a position to put a roof over her head and bread on her table, and perhaps word of her brother. Though she still wished her brother had come home as soon as she'd written him of their parents' death, the emptiness of his loss no longer seemed so consuming.

She had fled to London hoping to find a new future and a measure of freedom. Instead, she had found belonging and joy beyond her hopes. She had found a family. She had found love. The man of her dreams held her hand, and their wedding had been planned to take place three weeks from today. Nothing seemed too daunting to face—even meeting the Duke and Duchess of Charlemonte.

With Kit, she experienced the same bliss she'd known when playing the duet with him—a song of the heart they would compose all of their lives. Together, they would create a lifetime of sweet music, and so very many Sweet Memories.

Author's Notes:

Women's stays and corsets saving their lives is a well-documented fact. Due to the heavy, closely-woven fabric, folded and sewn in multiple layers, it creates a strong protection. Also, the center boning that ran vertically the length of the garment in front between the breasts was made of either a wooden slat or whalebone which would further deflect all but a very well-placed blow delivered by a strong arm. There are also reports through history of folded handkerchiefs, as well as small books such as bibles, saving lives from the deadly force of a blade or a bullet.

Contrary to what readers sometimes encounter in literature, a maid is not a proper chaperone; maids are servants who can be bribed or bullied. Only a respectable, mature woman who is married or widowed, or a spinster of good breeding and advanced years is considered a proper chaperone.

Since researching the working class musician proved more difficult than expected, I took some creative liberties combined with what I learned of Regency theatre and opera, along with my own experience as a theatre and music nerd in my youth. I hope the end result provided a satisfying, realistic-feeling Regency world.

The term bounty hunter was not in use during

the Regency, but it was common for people victimized of a crime to offer up a reward for the capture of the criminal. Some of these who sought the reward were honest lawmen, others were not so much.

For other books by this author, or for more information and to take place in contests, giveaways, and behind-the-scenes sneak peeks:

Website: www.donnahatch.com
Blog: www.donnahatch.com/blog
Connect on Facebook:
www.facebook.com/RomanceAuthorDonnaHatch/
Follow on Twitter: twitter.com/donnahatch

If you like this book, please help spread the word and rate it on Amazon, Goodreads, and other book review sites.

Thank you!

About the author:

Donna Hatch, author of the best-selling "Rogue Hearts Series," is a hopeless romantic and adventurer at heart, the force behind driving her to write and publish 14 historical titles, to date. She is a multi-award winner, a sought-after workshop presenter, and juggles multiple volunteer positions as well as her six children. A devoted music lover, she sings and plays the harp. Though a native of Arizona, she and her family recently transplanted to the Pacific Northwest where she and her husband of over twenty years are living proof that there really is a happily ever after.

Made in the USA
Coppell, TX
04 March 2020

16473229R00144